34-

THE SWALLOWED MAN

THE SWALLOWED MAN

EDWARD CAREY

THORNDIKE PRESS
A part of Gale, a Cengage Company

Copyright © 2021 by Edward Carey.

All images © Edward Carey except photographs of artwork by Edward Carey on pp. 18, 70, 99, 110, 125, 137 (top), 138, 144, 149, 173 © Nick Cabrera.

Thorndike Press, a part of Gale, a Cengage Company.

Thorndike Press® Large Print Basic.

The text of this Large Print edition is unabridged.

Other aspects of the book may vary from the original edition.

Set in 16 pt. Plantin.

LIBRARY OF CONGRESS CIP DATA ON FILE.
CATALOGUING IN PUBLICATION FOR THIS BOOK
IS AVAILABLE FROM THE LIBRARY OF CONGRESS.

ISBN-13: 978-1-4328-8798-8 (hardcover alk. paper)

Published in 2021 by arrangement with Riverhead Books, an imprint of Penguin Publishing Group, a division of Penguin Random House LLC.

Printed in Mexico
Print Number: 01   Print Year: 2021

In loving memory of my father
(1938–2010)
and my first son
(2006)

In loving memory of my father
(1938-2016)
and my first son
(2006)

1.

I am writing this account, in another man's book, by candlelight, inside the belly of a fish. I have been eaten. I have been eaten, yet I am living still.

I have tried to get out. I have made many attempts. But I must conclude that it is not possible. I am trapped within an enormous creature and am slowly being digested. I have found a strange place to exist, a cave between life and death. It is an unhappy miracle.

I am afraid of the dark.

The dark is coming for me.

I have candles; they are my small protection. And I have this purloined book that I shall slowly fill.

Before the last candle dies, I'll tell my tale. I give you fair warning: I can boast you no battlefields; this is no murderer's story; there is no great romance. But before all this, back on land, I did an extraordinary thing.

An impossible thing. And for that thing —
in order that the world may be put back in
balance — I am now paying a severe cost. I
shall tell my terrible shame, my tale of the
supernatural, though so devastatingly real.

Am I to account myself very fortunate, or
entirely devoid of luck? I considered myself,
before this last tumble, a very fortunate individual, blessed of more good luck, surely,
than was my fair portion. Back on land, after
all, I had made a miracle, I had fashioned an
impossible thing. But this piece of good luck
is overshadowed by a rather enormous piece
of bad luck that I am not quite able to forget,
for I live with the fact every day.

A monster-fish has swallowed me — a
shark or relative of that species, I am no
expert. It is no small basking shark that has
thus contained me, I say that straight, no
catfish with grand opinions of himself. I
have been taken by a colossus, perhaps the
largest of its kind that ever was. Perhaps the
last surviving *megalodon,* of prehistoric vin-
tage. Deep in such a thing do I dwell.

I had heard of this monster-beast, this
hunger-creature, ere I braved the waters.
Did I head out in a large military vessel
equipped with cannon and musket, with
harpoon and barbed hook? No, I must own

I did not. I set forth into the watery world on a dinghy, a rather ancient craft. It floated, it was seaworthy, so long as the sea was in good humor. I went out because someone had told me — was it a cruel joke, I wonder now? — that my own son was on the water in distress, and I wanted him back. I wanted, to be clear, to save him. But I did not save him. Of that, I am most keenly aware. I bought a small boat. It seemed a solid boat to me, but I am ignorant of such matters, and the farther I rowed, the less certain I was.

Some miles out, the water began to move strangely. Waves, when before it had been calm. My little boat rocking, soon some water spilling in. An increasing storm upon me. My little boat trembling more and more, and then waves breaking and the sea opening — as if it were boiling — and then the great mouth itself was upon me. The hole, rushing forward. The living tunnel hurtling unto me. Such a size, no hope against such a thing, like the world had erupted. The sea creature, colossus, flesh-mountain. I saw it only fleetingly, for a handful of seconds. Like Moses it split the water, and suddenly before me was a great black depth.

I fell, for there was no alternative, toward it and within it.

Into the very mouth.

I saw its teeth. Arranged in rows two or three deep. A graveyard.

On I fell, out and away from everything I knew.

Confined, constricted. Stolen!

How shall I ever find him now?

I shall never see him again.

I smashed down the dark tunnel, my body thrown and thumped, dashed and dragged, I was desperate for breath. Down and down, darker and damper, until at last the falling ceased. I had landed and now could breathe again. But what land was this, what peculiar geography? I was up to my knees in liquid. I puffed, I panted — I, somehow, *lived*! Scraped here and there, disheveled certainly, bruised and bloody, but still, no matter the unlikeliness, still alive. And yet what living could this be?

Rickety and miserable, harrowed by the dank rocking darkness, at last I started feeling about. The floor was moist yet solid enough, but even as I fumbled I could find no end to it. Timidly I rose, fully expecting my head to strike a surface, but soon I was standing at full height and still I found no roof. I lifted my shaking hands above me with caution, fully prepared for them to strike something solid. But the strike did not come. I proceeded to extend my height as well as I could and yet I touched only more unoccupied space. Only after a moment did rumors of the high ceiling begin to reach me, in the form of liquid dripping from above. I have suffered this small rain ever since.

Here, then, was space.

I set out east five paces, no limit; west ten paces, no end yet. The ground, I report, was not even. I tried to walk forward and stumbled upon objects, pieces of half-eaten sea life, yet still the place went on.

I called out, and the altered sound of my voice was a terror to me.

"Hallooo!"

The noise was unpleasant, and there came the response: *Hallo! Hallo! Hallo!* All the time quieter, the decreasing ghosts of my original sound.

I felt about further, in total darkness, no hint of anything but black and black and ever more of black, until I bumped into something solid. A wall, cast out at an angle, but not of flesh — it seemed to me, somehow, to be of *wood*. Planks of wood. Curving upward. Wood? Impossible!

I followed this wall with shaking hands and, finding its end, pulled myself up onto it. This took some doing, and I failed many times. But then — at the peak of its curve — a flat surface! Flat, here? Flat, true? Flat! It could not be. And yet it was.

I crawled upon this flat and had not been long about it when suddenly there was an opening in the flat ground and I tumbled downward, into something else. I had fallen again. Not so very far this time; about the height, I surmised, of a full-grown man. There was blood in my mouth. I felt about: more flat . . . and yet not only. I could not trust myself to believe it.

Stairs!

My hands discovered actual solid *stairs*.

No! Impossible! But there was no mistake. I had fallen down a set of stairs. Did this peculiar creature have perhaps a spiral stairway within its intestines? Was there an ornate rotunda to its heart? Twin outhouses of kidneys? Its esophagus a redbrick chimney flue? How strange, that a great fish should master the concept of right angles.

On the floor — solid floor, now, this was — I felt boxes, wooden crates spilled about. These were surely not a natural part of my enormous host, I sensed, but rather something consumable, like me. The lid of one I proceeded to break loose, then felt about its insides. Stacked in neat rows, I felt a particular column I was only too familiar with, made, I supposed — *O irony!* — of whale fat. Candles! Spermaceti pillars, so many night-killers, so many suns. And dry, by my word.

Hallo, tallow!

To light one and see again: how lovely that would be. I fumbled about, hoping to find a tinderbox to rescue me, but no such miracle was there. I was so thirsty to see again that I panicked myself utterly. Until in my weeping misery it at last occurred to me that I may have had the solution with me all along.

Joseph, Joseph, I said to myself, *have you ever been the smoker of a pipe?*

Aye, I answered myself, I am part of that fraternity. If there were light, I should show you my right index finger and thumb, be-yellowed by my habit. You would spy the evidence of a staining to the hairs of my upper lip. You would meet my teeth, also witnesses of this behavior.

So then.

Ah! Left trouser cupboard? Empty but for the leg. Right side: Something else there?

Careful now, careful, withdraw with steadiness. Is it there, I ask you?

Oh! It is, it is. Beautiful lady, Lucy, my Lucifer. So then, to strike the box of her, open her eyes.

I sent up a flare to heaven.

I lit my vesta.

I had light.

Light, ho!

It may have been a yellow, oily smear to you; it may have been hardly worth the effort; but to me it was the great flame of living. This flower, this beautiful ghost, this miracle of nature! I quickly applied match to candle, amplifying my illumination. I held aloft the flame and looked only into it. Oh, how I adored its darling warmth, its swinging form. I confess tears did prick me, and — good companion — it cried with me: the first splash of hot wax fell upon my hand. Here is light in my darkness, a whole crate of daylight for me. Seven crates in all.

Now I may fight against the night of the monster's belly.

I was in a small room, I learned now, a sort of antechamber, that much was plain. There were rooms east and west of me, incredibly, and there again were the stairs. I ascended them now with my fragile flame to better understand my situation.

Finally I comprehended that I stood upon a *ship.* By name *Maria,* from Copenhagen, it says on the stern and sides.

It seemed my capacious host, as if it were a fine hotelier anticipating my arrival, had set about to provide me accommodation. As it moved through the ocean, it had come upon a fishing schooner. Mistaking the ship for a marvelous morsel, it opened its drawbridge and swallowed the vessel whole.

And so, you see, I have a home. If you see my son, my love, my art, please have him write to me at my new address:

Giuseppe Lorenzini
The schooner Maria, *late of Copenhagen*
Inside the Beast Piscus Pesces
Mediterranean Sea

Her masts are three, mizzen, main and fore. All are cracked and splintered. The tallest reaches up to the ceiling of the creature and has wedged itself there, fish bone–like, and can never, I suppose, be unwedged again.

Here is my playground, my country, my scene. I have a forecastle, I boast me a poop deck and do stroll about upon the main. I lack not a quantity of soiled sailcloth. There are three hatches down into the ship, with berths within for eight or ten or twelve. There are hammocks and a captain's chart room, where this hallowed book was found, and beyond that his cabin. There are mess tables bolted to the floor in the galley. There is, in short, more space here than in the home I had before, for that place was in comparison rather limited — though I did prefer it.

But what space I have before me now! I am a monarch of space. Emperor of Inner Sharkland.

"Let slip, midshipmen," I call. "We sail! Hoist the mainsail!"

I have made me a model of my home, in gratitude, out of things purloined hereabouts, as though I might have occasion to sail it like a boy on a Sunday afternoon.

Can you imagine: a ship.

I am, despite everything, grateful to the *Maria*. For when my host swallows a deal of liquid — we are never dry in here — she lifts

16

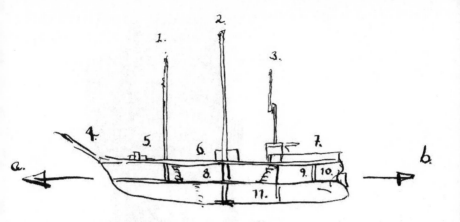

Key

a. to front of monster
b. to rear of monster

1. foremast
2. mainmast
3. mizzenmast
4. bowsprit

5. forecastle
6. main deck
7. poop
8. galley
9. captain's chart room
10. captain's quarters
11. water tanks

off the surface awhile and bobs and even tosses a little, from side to side, and in these brief moments of buoyancy I am kept safe by her, escaping the sudden drenching caused by the arrival of the latest great swallow. So then, this is sure fortune for me. And yet I wonder if the fact of the *Maria* is not in truth a piece of ill fate, since without her I should surely have been extinguished by now, and spared this watery purgatory.

I am, I suppose, being ungrateful. This

wood is good Danish wood, and I am its captain. And there are treasures to be found within *Maria*. May I tell you?

LIST OF LIFE

(Provisions found inside the good vessel Maria*)*

Tins of preserved meat
Hardtack
Bottles of wine
Raisins

18

Cheese
Coffee
Sugar
Tallow candles
Waxed matches

And in the bow of the ship, at the very bottom, are my life: the water tanks.

Here indeed is living.

And? Oh, happy discovery, this. This book. This journal. This sea captain's log come upon in a gloomy cabin. This tome in my tomb. So that I may write, and keep a little buoyant. Here, in this leather-bound volume found inside a desolate bark, I write my life. The history of my confinement.

There's not a dry spot in all this house. The walls are damp, the ceiling drips, the floor is moisture-laden. How careful I must be to protect this book from the encroaching wet. How often I have slipped — this is dangerous: I am not a young man — on this floor. The air here is thin and foul. It is rancid. Sometimes a new wave of stench comes in and affronts me. Sometimes the stink is but a whisper; at others it is a roar. But it always is a shade of stink.

Here, I am Josephus Odorous. Joey "the Kipper" Lorenzini. Putrefaction 'petto.

Should I ever happen to be set free — an unlikely thing, I know — I feel sure that no matter what soaps are used, what lavenders and rosemaries and flannels and brushes applied, no matter the personality of your talcum, the stench will never, ever leave me. Free though I might be, I shall still reek of imprisonment.

I reside, mostly, within the captain's cabin; it is my greatest pleasure. I have all the chattels of a captain, and am very shipshape. I do  pretend me a rank: Neither admiral nor commodore, I am but *Captain* Lorenzini. He has two rooms to himself, this captain does. A chart room with a table and nautical implements, and through a door the captain's cabin. The captain's bed is bolted to the floor, but it is attached to two large spindles that allow the bed to stay steady even as the ship sways with the sea. In that bed, even as the monster tosses, do I keep a kind of steadiness.

In the captain's cabin are various personal items that I have studied at length, though they were the captain's private company.

There is the captain's wine; I drink it, a little at a time, and toast his good health. There is a stuffed owl; it gave me such a turn when I first saw it, I nearly dropped my candle and lit myself and the ship. Why he went to sea with a deceased but preserved bird I cannot imagine: Sailors do travel with caged birds sometimes, for if anyone can find land for a lost ship it is a bird, but this is no live bird but an incontinent piece of taxidermy, whose owl shape slowly diminishes in favor of a pile of sawdust on the floor. I cannot explain the owl, but he does look at me, and I am a little discomfited by it.

But I have made other, greater discoveries: some paints, some colors, some tubes of rainbow. The captain painted! He was an amateur — a few of his pictures were left behind, and his portrait of a fish looks like an old person in distress — but I am so very glad of the paint. Here is also the captain's theodolite, though for me it gauges naught but the belly-roof, and his maps and charts, though not of this fish-country, and his compass, so that I always know the direction my prison is heading. O useless knowledge! We do travel, miles and miles, yet I never go anywhere.

There is, above all, this book, my captain's log. Great, beautiful, leather-bound. It has several pages written in it by the captain. I have left them there, and I study them with profound wonder. His name Harald Tugthus, his penmanship excellent, his words impressive, though what they mean I cannot say. Danish, you see, and I not a drop of Dane. All that was Tugthus is mine now. I am thief.

And so, in these pages, in this big book, I write this account of myself, for on the whole I would rather not suffer alone. I write it out for my son, for I am a proud father and I am also a considerable artist. With some strange piece of mighty good fortune, perhaps these words may one day be found, and be traced, perhaps, by digits other than my own. Should that happen, I pray you, my dear book rescuer, please read my account aloud to a great gathering, to all the people you know, or even deliver it in fond whispers to your maiden aunt, who is ill and perhaps lives at home with you. But please, great rescuer, living creature of sunlight and land, do me this favor, though you live far away: Tell my son. Do all you can to find him.

For, with all my achievements, I count this above every other:

I had a son.

Oftentimes, without quite knowing exactly what I am about, I become aware of myself holding some piece of *Maria* — hugging some beam or banister — and in so doing I have the dreaming notion that I have hold of my boy. I am made sensible always by the creeping knowledge that the wood is dead and makes no movement, being only still, lifeless wood.

My darling boy, wheresoe'er you are, keep away! The great fish seeks you out, I am certain. If you are yet on land, do not dip one woody toe into the ocean. Stay away from the sea!

My little lad.

Woodle.

I shall pour it all out in this book now. The tale of my son.

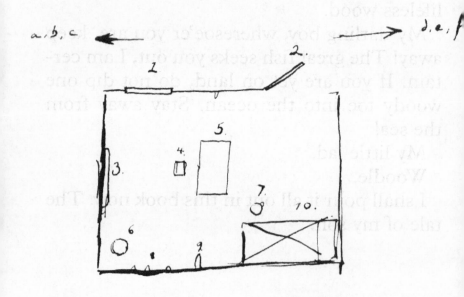

Key

a. to schoolhouse
b. to market square
c. to gaol
d. to church
e. to ceramics factory
f. to workhouse (oh, keep me from there)

1. window
2. door
3. mural
4. stool
5. table
6. bucket
7. chamber pot
8. hooks for possessions
9. gas sconce
10. bed

2.

I shall explain now how it came to pass.

The setting. Can you imagine: The small town of Collodi, province of Lucca, my home. Not much to it. A square with an equestrian statue in its center. The schoolhouse. Church. Baker. Butcher. Gaol. Graveyard. Two tailors. A failed ceramics factory. The workhouse. Population: seven hundred or thereabouts.

Can you imagine: A room. Here, I'll draw a map.

A single room, then, on the ground floor. A bed-sitting room. One window, four panes, top right cracked. One door out to the street — this will be important. On the west wall, a mural depicting a fireplace with a roaring fire. A pallet bed, not made, sheets not at their cleanest. Bucket. Chamber pot. Wooden stool, wooden table.

On the table: woodworkers' tools, clamp.

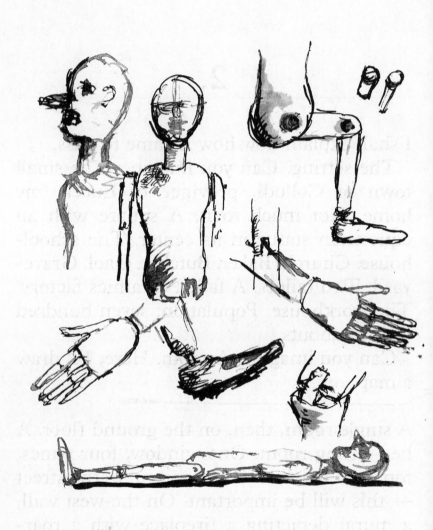

On the stool (4): me.
On the table (5): it.

He was not got in the usual way, my son. Before I tell you how it happened, let me prepare the ground just a little better: Have you ever had a doll that seemed to live? A toy soldier that appeared to have a will of its own? It is not so uncommon. So then, as you read, if you place that old doll or soldier beside you, perhaps that should help.

So to it:

I carved him. He came to me out of wood. Just an ordinary piece of wood.

I am a carpenter, to be clear. I had long desired to make a puppet, just such a puppet, so that I might tour all the world with him, or earn some little local money, or at least — I should say at most — to have at home a body, some company, besides my own. I had known bodies in my past; I was not always so singular. Yet I never did make a family of my own. Despite everything, despite my pride in my woodwork, despite the solid walls of my fine room, I confess I found my days limited in company. I wanted another life again, to make — as only a carpenter of my skill might make — the sacred human form in wood, for companionship, and to show off without question my very great worth.

I went about it in a creator's haze, in one of those moments when you are close to the divine, as if something of me and yet something altogether greater were connected to my feeble form as I worked. It was sacred magic.

Before long, I realized that something strange had happened.

The first glint came just after I carved the eyes. Those eyes! How they stared at me, directly, with intent. Perhaps I should have stopped there. Yes, I have been known to imagine things — like any other person — but this was different. The wooden eyes held their stare, and when I moved, they moved with me. I tried not to look. Are you, dear reader, an artist, even of the Sunday variety? Have you ever had those moments when, without quite knowing how, your art comes through with more grace, more life in it, than you had supposed possible? Have you wondered what guided your hand as you created this strange, wonderful thing? And have you attempted to repeat it, only to discover that it never happens quite the same way again?

I told you of this puppet's eyes: Staring eyes, unnerving eyes. But they were my work, after all, so I steeled myself and carved on. Next: A nose. And again, as I carved it, the nose seemed to sniff, to come living before me. To grow, you see, *long*. Longer than I should have chosen, but the wood, do you see, gave me no choice. It was as if the wood commanded me, not I it.

And then beneath, in a fever, I made the mouth. And this — oh, you must believe — this was the point of certainty! For the mouth made noise.

It laughed. It laughed . . . *at me*.

Nearly a boy's laugh, but not quite. A certain squeak to it.

This day was unlike any other.

I had never yet before made something living. But here it was! I went on, carving neck and shoulders, a little wooden belly. I could not stop. Arms! Hands for the arms! And the moment it had hands, this is the truth, they *moved*.

Have you ever seen a chair move on its own? Have you witnessed the promenade of a table, or seen knives and forks at dance with one another? A wheelbarrow wheel itself? Buttons leap to life? No, of course not. And yet we all know, we all have experienced, the disobedience of objects. And this object, mimicking as it did the rough shape of a body, presented itself to be a man! Right there and then. Before my eyes. It mocked humans; it mocked me.

Its first action, on finding movement: to pull the wig from my head.

I flinched; I shuddered. But it was too late to stop. I was in a passion of creation — I was under command of the wood — and so I carved on.

I gave him legs. Feet.

And the feet, on divining life, kicked with life. Kicked, that is, *my shins*.

This terrible thing!

You are an object! I cried. Behave like one!

And it kicked once more, for it was loath to follow the rules of objects. Rather, it threw down the book of rules and stamped upon it.

Oh *God*! I said to myself, for I was quite alone in my room. *What have I done!*

The thing moved.

I screamed in terror.

On finding it had legs, the thing had got up. It took to its feet, tested their balance, found them sturdy. And then it walked. To the door.

It opened the door. *And then it left.*

My sculpture, it ran. Away.

The thing was gone.

I screamed a moment and then I, too, ran. Terrified of losing it. For the thing was mine, it was my doing, I had made it.

Unlikely, you say? And yet it is all quite

true. As true as I am a man imprisoned inside a fish. I am being honest. I am rational. I am in absolute calm as I write, as I beg you: Imagine having an earthen mug for a son! Imagine a teaspoon daughter! Twins that are footstools!

It — the wooden creature, I mean; I did think it an *it* to begin with, forgive me — it did not understand. It had no comprehension of the world, or of its dangers. A shortcoming I discovered on the very first night of its life.

It had a voice, indeed it did. The next morning, when I returned home, it spoke to me.

Here I must add: That first night of its life, I had been forced to sleep elsewhere.

I had been, that is, locked up. Because I lost my temper.

That first evening, after I had carved it and lost it, I rushed out after it. I looked and looked, wondering at how this stick-thing could have escaped me, at whether what I'd lost was my wooden boy or perhaps, was this the truth, my own mind.

Then at last, in the street, there it was. The sight of it was so strange, so out of place in, of all places, the town of Collodi, province of Lucca. Yet there it was! I wondered how to approach it and settled on the most cautious course: I sneaked up behind it. And then, once my hands were upon it — one round its midsection, one clamped over its gouge of a mouth — I picked it up and turned for home.

But it struggled, the dreadful object. And *I* struggled, anxious not to lose it again. The wooden thing bit me, and I pulled my hand away. It shrieked out in great complaint. And I *bellowed*. I . . . said *words*. I was upset, you see. I was angry. I own that. I surely mimicked my own father that evening, my own lost father whose shouts still trouble me.

And then people came running and interfering, yes indeed, until onlookers and neighbors became a crowd. And the crowd said I was a mean man, and what awful cruelties would await my poor, though peculiar, child once we were both at home behind closed doors. It was the anger of love and of fear. The fury of protection! And then a policeman added himself to the crowd and put his ears to the situation. He was not without sentiment. And so my son — not fully comprehended in the darkness — was set free and I was taken to gaol. The people, the policeman, they sided with it! With *it*! It before me!

I was locked up.

Not because I was a precious object, not

32

to keep me safe, but because I was an unprecious object. To keep *them* safe. And so I spent the night confined. Disturbing the peace. As if my miracle were already polluting the morals of the world.

When I was set free that next morning from Collodi gaol — which has but two cells; we are generally a law-abiding folk — I rushed home. As soon as I reached my door, my rage flared up again. I suspected it would be home, I hoped it would be home. I meant to put it right, to make it known that I am a human and it but an object. The door to my home was locked. Indeed, locked by the creature inside.

I banged on the door. I banged on the window, in a fury by then. And looking in at the window I saw it: the carving, my carving! I tugged up the window and crawled in.

It spoke, its first word:

"Babbo!" That is how we say "father" in my part of the world.

Father!, it called me. The effrontery! Me, a real human. This object, this toy. It called me *Babbo!*

This little thing who refused to be a thing. Living dead thing. How it terrified.

And then I looked farther, down to its feet, and saw it: burnt stumps! It had set fire to itself. The flames were long extinguished, it sat in its own ash.

"You might have burned down the house," I told it, observing its scorched limbs. "The whole street."

"I was so cold!" it cried. "*That* gave me no warmth." It pointed to the wall, and I understood: The year before, on a cold night, I had painted a mural there, of a hearth with a pleasant fire. It was no real fireplace, for in my poverty I lacked such a luxury, but I had pretended one in paint — well enough that it gave me an impression of warmth on many nights, it fooled me very pleasantly. But it had not warmed the wooden thing, and the thing had resorted to making its own fire, a real fire, right in the middle of the room.

"You might have killed people! Burned down all Collodi!" I yelled. And paused, then, in wonder: "How is it that you speak?"

"I talk! Yes, this is talking. I like it. The taste of words in my mouth."

"Oh, terrible!" I said.

34

"But look at my feet! My feet are *gone!*"

"What a shame the flames climbed no higher," I replied, for I admit I was most upset. "What a shame you are not all ash. What trouble you cause, ungodly object!" Was I cruel to the creature? Put yourself in my shoes. (I, who once had shoes.) Who would not be? I weep for it now.

"I have no feet," it cried. "None at all. *No feet!*"

"Now where shall you run to?"

"Nowhere. I cannot!"

"It is your own fault. To play with fire! You are wood, you know! Remember that!"

"Daddy!"

"No! You are a thing, not a being," I told it. "Lines must be drawn."

"I am a boy," it creaked.

"No!"

"I am!"

"You are a toy, a wooden plaything. You are for people to use as they please, and then to put down as they please. No opinions for you. No complaints."

There was a silence then, a gap, until it screaked its question: *"How, then, may I be a boy?"*

"You may not. You must not consider it."

"I tell you I shall be. I wish it!"

"See there, object, see that hook there?

That is your hook. That is where you belong, alongside my tools and pieces. My mug. My pan."

My shaking hands. I found a screw eye.

"What is that?" it asked.

"This is a metal loop with a screw end, you see."

"What is it for?"

"It is most useful. If something has this attachment, then I can, for example, hang it from a hook. That hook there, for example. Turn around, please."

"What are you doing?"

"It shan't take but a moment."

I held him again, placed the end of the loop between his narrow shoulders.

"Ow! It hurts!"

"Come now."

"Ow!"

"A few more turns. There, then."

"What have you done to me?"

"Now you shall learn your place."

I heaved it up upon the hook and there it dangled. Kicking at the wall. Clack. Clack. Thump. Something like a hanged man.

"Let me down!"

"No, I shall not. Be silent."

"What a thing to do to your own son!"

"You are no son but a puppet."

"I am, Babbo. I am."

"Little boys go to school, little boys sleep in beds, little boys go to church, little boys climb trees. And you, doll, were a tree. Learn your place."

An hour later, having made certain the door was locked, I took it down. My hands were steadier then. I carved it new feet. I attached them with such care, with considerable expertise. You wouldn't know the difference. I am, you see, a god parochial.

"If you kick me," I said, "I shall keep you up there on your hook."

"I shall not kick. I have learned my lesson."

"Very good then."

"May I go outside?"

"You may not."

I lit my pipe. How it flinched at the flame upon my match. How shocked it was at the smoke coming from my pipe.

"Put it out! Put it out! We shall burn to death!"

"This fire, unlike yours," I said, "is safely contained within the bowl of my pipe."

I puffed.

"Look! Look at the weather!" it exclaimed.

I let free more smoke.

"What clouds! Do you make the clouds? Are you the one?"

How beautiful its observations! You see?

Yet then, as I heard them, I failed to appreciate.

"It is but my tobacco burning."

"I fear the flames."

"Be calm. It is but a small personal bonfire."

Later that day, I found it looking out the window, staring at the children rushing from the school.

"I wish to be a boy," it said. "To run like them, in company."

"We cannot have all that we wish."

"Do but look at them, Daddy! Hallo there! Hallo!"

"Come away from the window!"

I closed the shutters. It was a mistake to let it look out. It encouraged the notions.

"You embarrass me," I told it. "In front of all my neighbors, they who have proper children. Go find your hook."

"Why must I?"

"Because I tell you."

"And who are you to tell me?"

"The one who gave you life."

"If you gave it, then I'll take it. And I'll run with it."

"You'll do as you're told."

"Little boys don't sleep on hooks. Little boys have beds."

"Must I make a cot then for every pot and pan?"

"No, surely just for me."

The shutters shut up. We went about our lives, human and wooden. As I worked at my small carpentry, I let the thing play with odd little pieces I had in my possession. A list of his first friends:

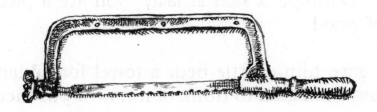

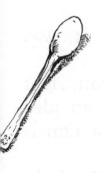

Ball
Bent spoon
Rusted chisel
Hammer
Blunted hacksaw

After a time, it was dark again, and we were both quieter. I looked over at it. It had grown so still that I thought it had reverted to its former life as a mere object. I thought it had lost the trick of movement. For a moment I was almost touched by this change, as if I should feel sadness instead of relief. But after a moment it spoke again; it could not stay silent forever; silence was not in its nature. At first I did not understand the noise, convinced it was the singing of my floorboards as I walked upon them — my weight, you see, giving them voice, not the boards calling out themselves. But then, as I readied myself for bed, I stopped moving, and still the creaking continued. I listened closer.

"Where shall I sleep then?" it was wondering.

"Sleep? You sleep where I place you, right there on your hook. Sleep! What an idea after all! You do not sleep. That action is reserved for animals."

Shriek. Such a shriek of wood. Words in the noise. *What am I then?*

"Branch," I said. "Twig. Treebit."

Such a crack.

Then, again, quieter: "What am I?"

And I thought: You are an impossible thing. Something gone wrong. A monster, I thought. O shame.

"Darling," I said at last, "you are a piece of wood."

I gave him a little bed, a towel for a blanket. I am glad to think of it now. I put them in a small wooden crate. It seemed happy with that, the odd thing. In time it closed its eyes. I watched it. I thought I saw its little chest upping and downing. Much easier to like, I thought, when it was silent and still. And I liked the sight so much that I picked up a pencil and drew it, while it was keeping still — as if it were an artist's lay figure, that relative of a shop mannequin. A counterfeit human. But I drew it as if it were a real child sleeping. A very fine piece of carving, I told myself. My best work. The more I was alone with it, even as it kept still, the more like a little boy it seemed. It was only later, when you put its face next to a real human one, that it failed to convince. Alone with it, you could almost believe.

What a thing I had done! What a creation. What woodlife. Suddenly I felt deeply pleased with myself, with this thing. I felt accomplished. Foolish man.

"I did that," I whispered.

Next day, I kept the door bolted again and the shutters closed. I was not ready to share it — whatever *it* was, exactly. How strange to find it still living when I woke. What a grand relief that was. It was playing with the small things I had lent it.

"I have been talking with the spoon," it said, shattering the peace. "I have had words with the hammer. I have confessed to the chisel. Listen up, I know your hacksaw."

"What are you saying?"

"They are hatching a plan, the things are."

"Are they now?"

"Most certainly. They are planning a revolt. Did you know, your own pencil disapproves of you?"

"It does not. It is merely a pencil."

"Yes! Yes! It has told me!"

"That is not true."

"The pencil has told me so himself. His name is Ernesto. He is but a portion of his former self, the poor pencil. He used to be much taller, I gather. You have made him so short with all your sharpening, haven't you? You have dwarfed poor Ernesto."

"It is a lie. You are lying."

"No, it's true," it said — and, as it spoke, something happened.

Upon the Good Book, an absolute truth, I promise it.

That nose — the nose of the thing, already prominent — it grew longer!

O disobedient wood! O unfamiliar life!

"True. True! TRUE!" the wooden bit continued, as if it had not noticed its nose's appalling progress, even as it advanced. I watched that nose stretch and increase until I thought it might touch the wall. It grew so much it started to imbalance the creature, to tip him over, nosefirst. What an abhorrence. What a vile root. Such an unwelcomed growing. It quite panicked me.

I stared at it, at that thing that should have had no life yet lived, and I screamed in my terror.

And in reaction — for terror is, you know, most contagious — the thing found a terror of its own. It screamed back at me.

Scream!

Scream!

"What's happening?" it cried.

"I can hardly say it. . . . Your nose!"

"Stop it. Please stop it!"

"I scarce know how."

"It feels bad."

"The wood was *dead*," I said. "I was certain of it. I cannot explain. To grow so many seasons in an instant!"

"Help! The strain of it!"

"It has stopped now, I think."

"But it is so long!"

"I could trim it, perhaps."

"Like Ernesto?"

"Thing," I asked — tentatively, now, for I was growing a great fear of objects. "Is the pencil's name truly Ernesto?'

"Yes. And the ball is called Elisabetta. She told me so."

The nose grew again. A hasty advance, reptilian, something stretching itself. Not natural, not in nature. *My dear fellow,* I said to myself, *you have come to life's end this very day. This whole room might grow branches,* I thought. *In time I may be more pierced than Saint Sebastian.*

And still it spoke on. That wooden thing, its life uncontained, sprouting forth excessively. It was an aberration, and yet — for I had been schooled in the Bible — it seemed something miraculous. No?

"The hammer is named Vittorio," it went on. "The pan is Violetta."

The nose, again. Progressing.

"Stop it! Stop it!" the mannequin cried.

"Is it true, my pine child? I wonder," I said, as I was beginning to reason something out for myself. "Can it be? Is this growth connected to your untruths? Each time you fib, your proboscis extends. Let us test it, shall we? So then: Have the objects, my object, been talking to you?"

"They have —" said the nose, creaking with life, stretching into branches, "— *not.* I made it up. I have no friends here. I gave them voice myself. I lied."

It stopped talking, and the nose stopped its journey.

44

"Ha! Ha!" I cried, for the truth had been discovered. Wonderful! "You must not lie, my little pine nut, for when you lie strange things happen. You keep lying like that, you'll end up buried in a plant pot. Upside down, with your head and nose-root deep in the soil."

"I must not lie," it told itself in utter fright.

"Or bad things will happen."

"I cannot move with such a snout! Make it go away, please, please, Daddy."

"Poor thing, like an antler grown in a moment. A nose antler."

"It hurts to have it. Please, Papa, what's to be done? Could you shorten it, like you did to Ernesto? Like the pencil, I mean."

"I may," I said.

I picked up a small saw and hacked away at his nose. The thing screamed, but I felt I must go on, though there was something unholy about it. I cut away at it and the longness was reduced. How large the eyes as the blade went fast and slow. I sanded down the new cut. There was a little drop of pine sap at the end; I dried it away with my handkerchief, though the stain has remained upon the cloth ever since. I applied fresh varnish. *There.*

"Now I am quite myself again," it said. And proceeded to prance around the room,

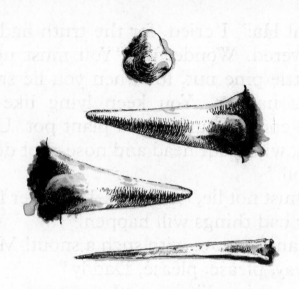

(My son's nose, and the tail of a
horseshoe crab found hereabouts.
The resemblance being noted by me.)

sending all the objects trembling. Then, as
it stomped its feet upon the boards — like
clogs they sounded — a plate of mine, made
by my own father, all indeed that I had left
of my father, came tumbling from its shelf
and smashed upon the floor. And that was
too far, that was all too much. With the
switch in my hand — a portion of its former
nose — I dragged the thing across my knee
and thrashed the stick upon the whelp until
there were marks upon his wooden back.

"That!" I said, pelting the object. "That
for lying! That for breaking the plate!"

At last I was too tired to go any further
and I must rest. I looked down at it. Pushed

it from my lap. The sight of the thing. Oh, the poor boy.

"Now we must shake hands," I said.

It looked uncertain.

"My father," I explained, "always insisted upon the shaking of hands after a beating."

"Your father did?"

"Yes."

"Well, then I understand, Babbo." And it took my hand. "A family tradition."

The poor thing had been very traumatized by its nose, I could see that now. It wanted to be close by me then. I took its hand and found it was not unpleasant; the wood warmed quickly in my grasp, until soon it felt indeed like a small human hand. I was taken in by it for a little time, even wondered what it might be like to be fond of a wooden boy. I contemplated whether I might refer to it as him. I was waking up.

Yet then it pushed too hard.

Of a sudden, it sat up and looked about. It was thinking. "There is more to life than this room," it said. "I think there must be. Don't you think so, Daddy?"

"It is our home," I said, struck.

"Small. Dim. Cold, too."

"You cannot know what I have gone through to earn this room."

"Unlock the door. I hear the schoolchildren!

Tell me, Babbo, for you of all people must know: How can I be a real boy?"

"You cannot."

"Come, I know I can. Teach me."

"It is a thing impossible."

"What is it children do? Tell me again."

"They run free. They fall and hurt themselves. And get up again. They make noise."

"Is that all?"

"I don't know." For I didn't. I was unfamiliar, by fear and by choice. "They are rude, I think. They shout. They do not like me."

"I believe that, poor Babbo. What else?"

"Fast — they are certainly fast. And filthy."

"Ah, I like the sound of it. I'll do it!"

"They come from woman."

"Every one?"

"Every one."

"Here is no woman."

"No. That is true. And so you are not, nor cannot be, a boy."

In the hours we had together, we played our game. At times, I allowed it. It liked that best of all.

"What is a human?" it asked.

"I am a human."

"Teach me to be one."

I could not convince it by words. I must show, I must demonstrate.

"If you're to be a child, you must sit up."

"There then." And it did it, creaked into position.

"That is the least of it. You must also be good. Or else the stick."

"Well, and what then?" it said.

"Say your prayers."

"I'll do it."

"Very well — let me hear you."

"Dear father, beloved Babbo, unhappy Daddy, please unlock the door. Amen."

"I can't let you out. You'll run away."

"I shall not. I promise."

I observed the nose. It moved not. To be certain, I measured it. Four inches and a little bit. Child.

We carried on with our game.

"Children go to school."

"Then I shall go to school."

"They learn their lessons."

"Then so shall I."

"It would be ridiculous!" I said, laughing at the idea. But look there: a seed growing in my head.

"I would like to try. Please, sir."

"You will run away."

"No, no, I shall not."

I observed. I measured. Inches four and a little bit.

"No," I said finally.

"Help me! You can help, sir. Father, you can, I know."

I could come up with no other response, so I did the only thing I could think of: I locked him in and I went outside. Where I could think. I was having ideas.

As I walked, I confess, I began to dream of money — a deal of money — that might suddenly be within reach. And why not? I deserved it, didn't I, after all these lean years? I was the maker, I alone. But first I had some things to do. To get more money you must start by investing a little, I thought, so I took my own coat down to Master Paoli's store — the greatest shop in all Collodi, almost anything may be purchased there — and sold it. With the money from the coat, I bought from Paoli some secondhand children's clothes, and something else: a schoolbook. And then, fool that I was, I carried them all home.

We clothe our children so they may fit in, do we not? I showed him the clothes and his wooden eyes seemed to grow. He reached out and put them on; a little baggy, but they fit well enough. The sight of him clothed made my eyes itch. So much more convincing wearing the pair of old shorts, the collarless shirt. How splendid to see a stick turning the pages of a schoolbook. Yes,

I thought, there was a trial: If I brought this woodlife to school, how would the children react? They'd not keep quiet, that was certain. They'd spread the news. The wooden child would become famous. First in Collodi, then throughout the world. And because of it, I too.

It would be the most wonderful business.

I had no understanding of the danger, not yet.

I took the screw eye from out of his back. "You no longer need this, my good boy." And so he — I began to call him *he* you see, I went that way at last — and so, yes, he would go into the world after all, this thing of mine, my mannequin.

"It is time for you to go to school, my little boy of pine."

"Father, what is my name? I should have a name if I'm going to school."

"Puppet."

"That is not a name."

Wooden monster, I thought. Haunted spirit begot from loneliness. Impossible life, miracle and curse. Specter stump. But I said, "Wood chip, wood louse, sawdust, shaving, lumberlife, kindling, pine pit — yes, there must be some pine, some Pino, in the name. Pinospero, Pinocido, Pinorizio, no, just plain Pino. Only pine, for that is you,

or for fondness, to add a nut, a *noce*. . . .
Pinocchio.

"Pinocchio?" he asked, excited.

"Yes, then, Pinocchio."

"Pinocchio!"

"It is time for school, Pinocchio."

"Goodbye, Babbo."

"Goodbye, Pinocchio."

I opened the door, how the light rushed in through the oblong, and I watched him walk out into the world. To see him so

illuminated! Down the street he went, out of my reach, toward the schoolhouse.

I watched the breeze ruffle his clothes, as if the wind itself supposed he was one of us. To think I had made such a creature, that set forth this way on its own feet! *How well,* I thought, I shall be known for it. *How celebrated — the creator of life. I shall be rich, I think.* I watched him go, his wooden gait, his upright form trying to be flesh. What a thing. He walked as if he belonged to the world. I did not call him back, and off he creaked, as I watched. It quite broke my heart. To see him so excited, with his schoolbook, as if he were equal to any other. Off, impossible thing! Yes, off to school.

And he never came back.

How I waited. But he never. I'd lost my life. All company gone.

I have not seen him since. Unless in a dream be counted.

Though I dedicate my life to recovering him.

The school day ended, and my nightmare began.

I waited, as I say, but the wooden boy never returned. I looked out the window. Time after time I arose from my chair and nearly set out the door, stopped only when

I thought of how I might sound to others. *Have you seen my boy? He is a stick, a carving, a puppet.* So I sat in silence, hoping for his return.

A few hours later, unable to wait any longer, I set out at last to find my wooden child. I went to the school, but he was not there, of course. Nor had he ever been. Nor was he in any of the nearby streets, nor anywhere in all Collodi. My panic mounted. I kept imagining him hiding behind a tree. The sight of a branch made my heart beat faster. But it was never him.

So then I must go farther. Beyond the walls of our town, high and low, I sought my son. Yes, I had begun to call him that then, I had come that far. Please, have you seen? A boy, my wooden boy? Wooden? You mean that he has a wooden leg? they replied. Poor thing! No, no, I said, he is wooden top to toe. How I was laughed at, mocked from place to place.

"It — *he,*" I said, "belongs to me. I made him. I carved him. My finest work."

"Sculpture is it, now?"

"Yes, yes," I said again and over. "Mine. My doing. My darling."

"It got up, then, you say?" said the person beginning to understand. "Your handiwork did, and it fled?"

54

"Well, yes, it could be put that way — or it may have gotten lost."

"What state must a man be in, to be convinced that his own things desert him!" The people would not believe me.

"He has gone out on his own, without permission, my sculpture. I demand him back."

And on it went, from town to town. Word spread of my mania; some towns it reached before I did myself. Mad Joe, they called me. But I was not. I was so sure of him, the wooden child.

To be fair, not everyone laughed at me.

"Such a phenomenon," said one old fishwife, a wrinkled piece of life who showed the kindness to listen to me. "It's the days we live in. Do you know there has been spotted off the coast an enormous shark? The size of a city hall. Yes, yes, it's the days we live in."

"I'm not talking about a shark!"

"Perhaps tomorrow the world will cease."

She had at least listened.

Yes, that was when I first heard of the great sea creature. It was called at times shark, at others whale. People had seen it. The monster thing. I heard of it now and then, so often as I roamed, that I wondered if it was somehow connected to the wooden boy. The unnatural child had so thrown the world off-balance that it must be righted at any cost, and perhaps the only thing with the power to right it was a gigantic sea monster, born — I began to suppose this — just after I cracked the world by making a wooden person. Perhaps, in that small window of miracles, this gross leviathan had also been hatched, born to rid my son out of this world and thus put right the wrong I had created. Such were my thoughts. A sea monster! I believed it. Indeed, I was certain of it.

I stayed inland. I prayed the woodenlife would leave the ocean alone. Yet more and more I heard it mentioned: the seabeast, the sharkfort, the whalecastle.

On I looked for my boy. Town and city. And as I walked, finally, I began to pick up news of a strange child seen here and thereabouts. Like Kaspar Hauser, the feral boy of Nuremberg, stumbling into the town square, only this one carved of pine. It made the people gasp. Perhaps some screamed as I had done.

But never came I close to him again. Until one day:

"Yes, I have seen just such a one! A wooden boy — so high?" This from a master puppeteer with a black beard, holding his hand at stomach level to indicate the boy's height.

"Truly? Truly?"

"Yes, yes, he was here."

"He is mine, you see," I said, the tears coming though I hated them to. "I made him. But I have lost him. Where is he? Show me swift."

"He is not here, old man. No, not for weeks and months."

"Not here again. My boy."

"I have many other puppets," the puppeteer said, reading my sorrow.

"No, him! I need him! Not one of your lifeless stringfellows. None other like him. My greatest work."

"He was going home," the puppet master said. "That's what the puppet said, in any case. To see his father."

"Did he? Was he? He missed me? A good boy, then! Isn't he? Though so wooden."

I rushed home. It took me days. I felt sure I'd find him there, and if I did, I swore I'd never let him free again.

But he was not home, though I searched the place. It did not take long. Four corners.

I could not free my mind of the wooden-life. I went out again, sometimes returning home just in case, but never was he there. At home I tried again at carving a wooden boy, a new one, but the results were all failures. Lifeless mediocrities. Then off I went, my search renewed.

■ ■ ■ ■

And so, at last, I found myself upon the coast — at the very end of land, somewhere I had not been brave enough to look yet, somewhere I feared to go. There I stood, at the sea, having lately heard report of an unnatural wooden thing that had been troubling the town — "an automaton," one bill poster called it. I reproduce the poster here to the best of my ability.

The people had called the wooden child heathen, I gathered, unholy, the devil's work. They had chased it until finally it was captured, tied it up, and cast it adrift upon some ancient tub.

"You threw him in the water?" I cried to a boasting fisherman.

"It was such a strange thing, you'd flinch at the sight of it."

"A child — you did this to a child? Tossed him to the ocean?"

"Well . . . well," stumbled the man.

"A little boy so lost on the waves!"

"He is made of wood, see, so must float, I suppose."

"Wretched people, have you no love for life? No, no, you'll drown it all. A little boy set adrift!"

"He did come back once, sir, with the

tide," admitted the fisherman, staring down at his feet.

"And what did you then?"

"Shoved him off again, forbade him to land."

"Oh, you are the monsters! My own little boy."

"He was not one of us, you do see that."

"He may be of wood, but you are made of stone. Have you no feeling? Ugly people, miracle-murderers."

And so I had no choice: I must set out myself onto the uncertain surface.

Buying a small vessel, from a different fishing fellow, I launched into the water. And then, you see, it came to pass — I had my fall into darkness.

And so I am here, stuck here. Where I can never find him. Nor hope for my return. No help. No rescue.

There, I have told you. How a father lost his wooden boy.

3.

New things are delivered to me here every day through the mouth of the great fish. Mostly I have in the post: shells and fish and sea-meat of every kind. And amidst it all, from time to time, come other small things that tell of humankind. Little shards of smoothed glass, or even, now and then, O wonder, small pieces of broken porcelain that the great beast has bothered up from the ocean floor.

But not yet my child, not all of these todays.

Still, the shark looks for him, I feel certain of it. What other purpose for this great monster?

For example, it sometimes — rare times, but still — delivers me wood. This is close to him, not yet him but getting warmer. Wood! *Hallo, you were a tree!* I call, *I was once a human.* I have been wave-battered and sea-scrubbed, sea-weeded, salted, dripped and dropped and pickled here, but once, I cannot quite say how long ago, but yes indeed I was once . . . a fellow.

I feel such sympathy, now, for ships in bottles. I know you, my friends. I do live your story. What horror, the cork going in. It is very thin air inside, is it not? Oh my darlings, would that I could pull out the stoppers and see you all float free. What an armada!

As long as I have light, I have life. When the last candle is gone, the last match struck, then am I in misery locked. For there is no light from the gill shutters of this shark, or at least none that reaches me here. Nor do I have, as the Pantheon of Rome boasts, a blowhole in my roof. How nice that should be — news from above! But the darkness is, I am afraid, total. How I feel the dark. In the darkness there is just my heartbeat, no other trace of me. I know now that I can put it out, but not forever. What then?

Ever since losing my Pino I have begun to look differently at objects. Wondering if they have life, too. At times, these days, I feel more at ease with a fishing net than I might be with a fisherman. That I might be companion more to tin than to tinsmith. That I would be closer to needle than to needlewoman. Have I been demoted? Do I yet count?

Am I growing wiser, I wonder, as I am being punished?

Sometimes, as I drift off to sleep in the dark, my own father comes back to me. *Babbo.* I am not frightened of him any longer. Sometimes in this watery tomb I hear him sighing. He is put off by me, I know. Irked that I am here when I should not be. No, no, he would be distressed. He would cry, I know, to see me come so old, so white.

My own dear Babbo was all Industry. I, his boy, was entirely Idleness. Our family business was painting upon pottery: We provided decoration for plates, for oil jugs, for pots and cups and what have you. It was family tradition, the painting of this on that. In my childhood, his factory was the most famous business in all Collodi. At one time employing a full thirty people.

The paints were always the same, the pattern ever identical. It was the family pattern, you see, it was our birthright. And, from my earliest scrawling, I too was directed to practice this same pattern upon paper — always and only this pattern — until I had proven my manhood by mastering it. On the day when I had at last got it down, and only then, I would come into my own. Yet I never could quite perfect it. It taunted me in my sleep, this design, tried to etch its curves onto my skin, to tattoo me with itself. How that pattern persecuted me. It was the family fortune. I must draw it every day.

Each morning, Father would look over my shoulder to inspect my painting. Five times through the course of the day, at the very least, he returned to look again. And every time he would render the same verdict:

"No. No. Not yet. Look again."

Or, "It is not right."

Sometimes, even, "You do this, I am sure, to insult me."

But I never got it right. Some children are given lines to write out (*I am a willful and ignorant child,* one thousand times), but my endless punishment was that pottery pattern. Beautiful, you may say, as many do, but to me it was murder. No other creation but this, no other colors or lines or curves or bursts, until it did me over. I could not devote myself to the same four-petaled central flower, to the smaller five-petaled flowers that framed it, to the meaningless lines between them. This same design repeated again and again, as if it were the only choice. But every day burnt sienna, straw yellow, violet, and burgundy. I yearned for turquoise, the pattern not containing any; I called for cobalt; in my sleep I screamed out *periwinkle*! And when I dared to draw or paint something other, my father would find it out (he had such a nose for it!), rip it up, and shine his anger upon me.

"Cruel!" I would be called.

Sometimes, even, "False child."

All this because I could not learn the family language.

I was very good at school, top of my class in Collodi. I did not mess about like my friend Antonio and the other boys; rather I liked the books, liked to get lost in them. The teacher even ventured that one day I might go to university.

My father said no I would not. All the learning I needed was at home, in the pattern.

This is what my family looked like, a portrait of a people:

Actually, that is not bad at all! Father, Father, do but look. What say you?

I can almost hear him: *My boy, my only boy! Look how you keep the family. So proud, boy!*

But no, he did not say that, not ever.

It was my great-great-grandfather Giambattista who started this curse, he who founded our family business, once Collodi's most prosperous. It was he who devised that pattern, one so striking, so beautiful, so perfect that to paint any other was to shame the family. It was what we were known for. All we ever were.

Were Father to have gone blind, I think it would have been of no great matter; he surely could have painted the pattern, so well did it fit him, without requiring his eyes. His apprentice boys managed to pick it up in a few months. But I, who had spent so many years at it, never could. Father, though he loved me, loved me a little less because of it. Indeed, I think he struggled over what was the point of me. There was only one labor, for this family, for this town.

And yet, as I grew up, I started whittling — started making my many woodthings. In private I found this other way of communicating. I had a simple penknife, and as I walked the woods around Collodi, I took a dead branch from an old oak and made a little face in it. That was how it started. I brought the little work home.

Father greeted it as a crooked thing for me to have done. To him it smelled of betrayal. But I could not stop myself. I carved little things in wood, strange faces, odd creatures, letting the wood guide me. And then, when I returned to the painting of pottery, my

whittling thoughts came along with me. I took the pattern of my family's fortune and changed it; I pushed the pattern, pulled it, stretched it. I let the brush guide me. Sometimes I feared that I had broken it altogether.

If here I seem to exaggerate — and I confess that I do, somewhat — it was as if I had made such a mess.

"Why, why, why must you?" called my *babbo*. "Oh, my God, how have I upset you so that you send me this doltish donkey for a progeny? You mock me, my boy. You mock kith and kin, you mock bread and wine, mock father, mock love."

"No, Babbo! No, sir. No, truly."

"Yes, boy, you do."

"I do not mean —"

"Then paint the pattern as it has always been."

"Now, Babbo?"

"This very instant."

I picked up a plate and did what I could. He took it from me and broke it, Father did, as if he were terrified that someone might witness our family come to ruin.

Father, O Babbo, please forgive?

I seem to hear him now, here in the whale: "My son, my only son, do not let the pattern die. The pattern. Oh, the pattern!"

Father, I have a son of my own now, or had. A little wooden life.

Father, O my *babbo,* do but look at me now. Your Geppetto.

Today I shall paint a sky, lest I forget it. I shall hang my little piece of blue upon the wall and call it a window. See, I look out: sky light.

Geppetto

I know there is sky above me, but between me and it there is so much living, undulating wall. These walls — or one continuous wall? — are so thick. How to pull them down, how to make a hole? I shall further think on it.

I imagine billowed clouds, plump like breasts, rolling in a light blue sky — a canopy full of them, but with some darkness. Perhaps later on it shall rain. Wind, too, I think. Autumnal weather. The first coolness after summer.

I have here with me — it came in the post some while back — a large bone. Perhaps once a hip, perhaps in fact a shoulder. What creature, whether the former property of a whale or even of a cow that somehow unlucked into the salty wet, I cannot tell. Whoever it was that left me this flat field, I heartily thank you, for your life and for your death, for now this piece of you has given me a solid surface to work on — not paper, which is ever in danger of damage, but something as close to rock as ever living creature made. Upon this solid surface, little land that it is, I shall paint me a skyscape in precious oil paint and call it *Joseph's*

Window. I'll hang it here in the cabin, and look out of it often. (Though in truth I am looking onto it, still I shall lie it my way.)

I have about me some treasure from my Collodi life. I carry, always around my neck, carefully preserved, daily felt between shirt and skin, a miniature likeness. At my bedtime I take it out and place it upon the ledge where Captain Tugthus nailed his two photographs of his people. My miniature was drawn from life, upon a little oval of vellum (the skin of a goat in this case, not a calf), as much of it as I could afford. I should have liked to make it a large portrait, like one of those mammoth equestrians. It should have been as large and as grand as the field of canvas taken up by kings, for then indeed it would have boasted accurately the size of my achievement. But it is a likeness, small but true — and that is the certain point. A plumbago portrait, in glorious graphite, of my child, my son. It is sketched with such small sharpness, a portable likeness of the little fellow, taken from life. Though among the smallest, it is yet the principal object in this museum of mine. Yes, there he is, a boy: my boy.

His eyes are closed, as you observe. No, he is not dead; this is no death portrait, no postmortem likeness. I forbid the thought of that. No, it is taken from life. And I must confess: I took this likeness without his permission, before he left me. While he was sleeping. The wood seemed so still, as if he had no idea of movement, so I drew him, O forgive me, as if he were a flesh one, like all the others. A true boy.

To put it clearly, I unobjected him. Can you object to that?

Hushed and busy in candlelight, I put him — adapted so, so tenderly — upon this vellum, this piece of animal flesh, so that his image should be with me always. Look! He would never sit still, never could for a moment, such a fidget he was. Not to be confined, not by room or by house. He was born to hurtle out of his chair, out from his first beginnings — out into town, out into countryside. What a traveler, a wanderer, an itch, as if to keep still would be a declaration of death. There he is! Look at him! I made him! Boy!

How the world would have flocked to him, if only they had known.

Such a living he might have given me.

A fortune I might have made.

Do but look.

And not only this sacred likeness, but also something other. Small yet considerable. Consider, if it helps, how people do go about cutting small bushels of their beloved's hair and keep these among their most prized

possessions. Here he was, they say, and here she was; hair from his head, hair that she grew; ah, my grown darling, oh, my gone darling. They did this, I have learned, with the French king Louis and the British king Charles after their heads were struck off, that in death some lasting proof would be daily kept. But I am not talking of kings, only of ordinary folk with ordinary feelings.

Do but look. Here I have, right here in this tin — I fear to touch it, lest I should lose it — a chip of wood. A piece of him.

4.

I have no way to measure it, but I am certain the weather here is very nearly constant. Seasons have perhaps come and gone since I arrived, but I have no experience of them. The sun is quite dead to me.

It is all too masculine, here in the swallowed ship. And in such a place, one's mind naturally turns, how could it not, to the women.

I was once, by accident, a prodigy in the matter. At first I was shy of females, observing at distances, avoiding contact. *Until.*

A list of the small connections I had before at last — at my advanced age, in my unusual way — I became a father.

Agnese
Sylvestra
Jacopa
Antonella
(Laura)

That is the list. No Don Juan then? No, perhaps not. Nor exactly a Casanova.

Here, in my dark place, I do my best to remember my lost loves. Dances of mine. Small intimacies. But to have them down as they should be. I shall struggle at this, in paint a little — not from life, alas, but from what I can pluck from memory.

Inside the cavern of my predicament, floating here and there upon the surface, are to be found small pieces of wood that have been pebbled by the sea. Has the cruel water chewed at my son now, have the waves worn him down, is he still lost in the seas? Thrown by tempest so many miles? Or has he come home at last and waits for me in the old four corners? I cannot say. But these wooden crumbs are not him. These small bits have been spun and thrown, heaved and dropped, sucked and gobbed by oceans, until all the edge has been licked off them,

leaving them most pleasing in shape and feel. Upon five of these sea lozenges, I have affixed with brush my history of love. For I did love before the wooden prodigal, yes, I did. And this is a story of love, is it not?

I am, by nature, somewhat timid. I crept about in the background of life, quietly breathing the shadows, avoiding the taste of stronger light. I supposed my life would be one of observation only, of taking notes of the smaller events, events that other people should never even consider events. I was in the business of finding the mundane marvelous. I praised the sparrow and the daisy. A pigeon's coo: a thunderclap. My odyssey was to the greengrocer's, my famous battle a visit to the butcher. My king was the local policeman. But I took all I saw, all the little things, and carried them home with me; I nibbled at human relationships; a brief nod would sustain me all day. A slap on the back would keep me smiling for weeks.

I was so deeply retiring, in short, that I might have disappeared altogether, were it not that I am — despite my father's deepest wishes — a carpenter. My art is bolder than I. It sends messages of me out into the world. When I am with wood and we work together, things come out of me that I should never have thought possible.

From the start, I have found it easier to be brave with wood. As a young man, I busied myself constantly making little things, small fancies: a tiny house, dodos, lizards, dolphins, porpoises, krakens, hydras, dragons, all kinds of beasts in wood. Unlikely worlds come to me through pine. I do see fairies in wood where, I think, other people see just kindling. And so I was compelled to bring the fairy out so that all, at last, may see it. There are strange creatures everywhere; I summoned them in whittling in the privacy of my bedroom. What fancy I had in my childhood, what openness for the unlikely, I redden at it now. Such wonderments I shunned from my adult life. Casting all away, embracing the only true life, the real and austere. It was better that way: I was full-grown.

Short of funds — as my father refused me even pocket money until I had mastered the pattern — and deep in distress, as a youth I took these small oddities I had made, my first children, to the Collodi market. At the far edge of the throng, and nigh-on invisible in the shadow of a large bronze horseman, I cautiously sold my wares. The statue was of Ottavio Garzoni, patriarch of the wealthiest family in this region: a fine model of a mounted gentleman, the ideal human on the ideal horse. The same figure is to be found in several of our local squares; indeed, for many years I thought it was mandatory that all town squares possess one. It was here, in the gloom cast by the huge horseman, that I found my place.

I would lay out my large handkerchief, position my small wooden suggestions upon it, and so sit without ever calling for attention. I did not boast like the chicken-sellers, for example; I did not scream on behalf of roasted chestnuts; and oh, the vendors of olives and cheese are a loud breed. I sat on in silence, quiet beneath the statue, hoping a little that none should come by, that I might take my makings home again and keep their company a little longer.

It was one day, as I was thus situated, that the occasion occasioned.

Agnese.

Oh, Agnese.

She was small and she was very fair. Her hair was almost white, her eyelashes too, and her eyes were blue. A mole upon her chin. Small freckles around her nose. She was a butcher's daughter. She wore big boots; I believe they had belonged to her

78

brother, who had lost his life tumbling down a dry well. (How we tumble, we humans.)

I was gazing down at my works, when suddenly her boot was on my handkerchief.

"What's all this, then?" says she.

I could not but be silent; I feared that I should cry.

"Are you having a picnic?"

"N-n-n-n-o. No indeed."

"They do not look comestible."

"No, and are not, surely."

"What then?"

"They are, so please you, little people," I ventured. "Small creatures of science and imagination. Made of wood."

"Yes, they are! Did you make them? Are they your fault?"

"I did, yes. All my own."

"May I pick one up?"

"Oh, truly! Will you be careful?"

She scooped up a creature.

"What devil is this one then?"

"It is an elephant seal."

"You thought this up?"

"No, so please you, it is a real thing to be found in the ocean."

"You saw one?"

"No, I never. Not in life, but in a book at school, when I went to school, there was one. I saw that."

"It makes me smile."

"It does? Does it?"

"I'll buy it, I think. I don't know what to do with it, mind. It's not what you would call useful." How sharp her words. *Not what you would call useful.* "But there's something to it. I tell you what: it has a spirit."

"Oh. Yes. Well. I do thank you for noticing that. I am made very glad by it."

"What a strange creature you are. I can't see you properly there in the shadow, come out a bit. Let me have a good look."

"Oh. Ah."

"Come on, shift."

"Here I am."

"Yes, there you are at last."

She stood staring at me out in the light. Until it grew too much.

"Can I go back now? If you don't mind."

"No, no, you may not. Stay where you are."

"Oh, dear."

"There's not much to you, is there?"

"Barely anything at all, I shouldn't wonder."

"Tell you what, I like you well enough."

"Oh. Thank you!"

"You should eat more meat. How much do you eat, then?"

"Oh, not very much at all."

"I knew it. You should eat more."

"I am to have more meat once I have

80

mastered the pattern — our family business, that is. Meat, you see, is, on the whole, costly."

"It is. Well, I'll cut you some meat. Some meat for the creature. What do you say? Shall we shake on it?"

We shook on it. Her hand in mine. So many Sundays all at once. That was how it began. With a little wooden figure of an elephant seal and some cuts of pig.

Over time, one market day after another — I measured my life then in market days — she bought the lot.

We would meet up, it was her suggestion I need hardly say, at the local cemetery, very near to the Collodi church of Saint Bartolomeo, who is the patron saint of butchers and tanners and bookbinders and who was flayed alive. There she would give me, wrapped in yesterday's newspaper, small trinkets of meat.

"Here," she would say, "pork chop."

On another day she might say "Tenderloin," tenderly.

Or, less formally, "Rump."

I took these wrapped payments and placed them beside me.

She smelt a little of her meat, did Agnese, of the butcher's business. I didn't mind, no,

I liked it. There was not much courting, not much talking, not in the beginning. After only a few such meetings, I suddenly found her lips upon mine. It was a little surprising to me, but I liked it very much. She laid me down in the graveyard grass with all the dead beneath us, and with some cut of animal wrapped in paper beside us, and she put her lips to mine. Her lips to these lips. I was shaking, rather, though it was not cold.

"I mean to kiss you," she said.

!

"Oy, now kiss back, won't you? It's not good if I'm the only one at it."

So.

How's that? Was that all right? Oh, what does she think of it?

"Better. You haven't done much of this, have you?"

"Not oft, I must allow."

"No, me neither, in truth. But I'm interested and want to learn. And I thought, you know, I thought of you, you're there and here I am."

I was there!

Only this cry: I am still here!

We were found out. It was the undertaker's son Alberto Crespi who saw us, saw us on the graveyard ground with dear Agnese beneath me. A little loving parcel of sweetbreads beside us. We heard a gasp. But did not see him. And he told: ran with the story to his father, the undertaker, and that undertaker undertook the story to my father, and also to Agnese's father, the Collodi butcher, and what butchering there was then. What spillage of porcelain, how like a butcher to break my father's work in his fury. What a fortune was lost that day. So much destruction that my father's business was in peril. My fault, I must own that.

From that point forward, I was forbidden to see her. I was forbidden to leave the house, for that matter, forced to stay inside within pottery limits. Never to go to market. Never to whittle no more. I was specifically warned to cast aside all thought of wood-carving — for surely, he raged, this was the cause of my straying and straining. *And in the churchyard!* he bellowed. *Sin upon sin!*

And Agnese? Oh, Agnese. I read later, in the newspaper, that she married the son of an abattoir from the nearby city of Pescia. Listen to me: No child is born from an abattoir! For that place takes life, not creates it. No, no, I mean the abattoir owner's son, one Ludovico Donati. In his blood did she mix, with his meat.

She was my first love. We were famous

explorers, we two. But we were separated and dragged back to our separate family terrains, each a distant island one from the other. The space between us, a no-man's-land.

Then came Sylvestra. I was never equal to Sylvestra. She appeared in my life after she had had a personal fall, otherwise I would not have known her.

She was, for a term, Father's secretary. She was imprisoned inside our house, poor girl, on account of some business concerning a mustachioed lieutenant.

So, for a short term, we were both at gaol in my home, I for Agnese and she for her lieutenant. And even as I strove to repeat the family pattern — and there was an urgency to it then, so much inventory had been lost — so did Sylvestra worry over the ledgers in the family office. Her days were all numbers, and this gave her no pleasure; the numbers dried up her skin and made her look lopsided. She slept in the little office; I toiled nearby in the workroom, struggling with the glaze. And at times she came to me, and sat beside me very close, strangely close, and looked at me. And talked a little of what life there was beyond our closed walls. She longed to run out, she said. What shall we do? she wondered to me. Sometimes, in her frustration, she would let me touch her and admire her. She was, perhaps, ten years my senior. She was, I think, not at all happy. Later she chose a different worker to talk to, the last of the strong young men Father employed after letting the others go, and she did not sit by me again. Sometimes, when she talked to Father, I saw her touch his elbow. And once he leaned out to touch her and she smiled at him. Finally, one day, her mother came to collect her, and Father was in a hot temper and she was gone. I never quite knew what to make of her, nor what Father had done to provoke her departure.

So then, in due time, Jacopa. Ah, Jacopa. There you are now. I am sorry that you look so ill again. It would have been kinder to portrait you looking well, though it would be a lie. I could have cured you with watercolor paint. But I was unable to do it. And you come out again on this curved driftwood, yellow of skin, pale, smelling, my darling, of your disease. What a character that disease was, how it tried to assert itself over you. But you would not stand for it! In your wrestling, you would come out on top, outdoing it with your good spirits. Jacopa, I am so sorry at your going. In paint and ink, let me tell you of you.

Jacopa, taller than me. Jacopie, oh, Jacopie, such length and sorrow.

We worked together, Jacopa and I. After Father had died, and the business was ruined, I found work with the Capuchin monks in distant Palermo. I crossed — how it horrified me then, though I laugh at it now — the little Strait of Messina, which seemed to me such an eternity, though it took not quite an hour of passage. From there I trekked to Palermo, where I took work that all others shunned, carving niches for the dead. I was with death then a great deal.

Jacopa loved the dead. She was a mother to them.

In the monastery, beneath the ground where most people are buried, in the great cellar, was kept the city's great pride: the resting places of the expensive dead. This may sound no different from anywhere else, but let me make clear: these dead were stored vertically, not horizontally, and not within boxes, but out for all to see. These dead stood in their Sunday clothes, upright. I was the person who carved their niches and strapped them in to keep them standing. Jacopa was the one who helped preserve the bodies, so that even though they were dead they might look less so. Thousands of the dead were kept there, for the living to visit. And the dead were sorted: there were rooms for monks, rooms for doctors, rooms for women, rooms for the children. There were two methods for dealing with the dead people. The first was to stand them up in the cellar in a closed chamber and let them drain naturally, and then, after a year, to wash them in vinegar and thence to dress them and have them displayed. The second method — and here my Jacopa was especially attentive — was to bathe the dead in arsenic. And in this way, do you see, she was too intimate with them. They got to her, in the end, the dead did. They were too numerous, and she was too close.

I would not say Jacopa's dead looked alive, exactly. I do know the difference between alive and dead. Rather, they looked somewhere in between. Like dolls, perhaps. But very individual dolls. In that place, it was a great privilege to be buried standing up in such smart clothes. People used to come and see these dead all the time, and others who were shortly to die, or thought they were, would come along and stand in the niches — to practice, I suppose, for the afterlife. How still the dead were, after I had strapped them in so well.

I made other repairs about the monastery, I fixed pews and carved new faces on them, replacing old rotten wood, but mostly it was the dead cellar I liked to be in, on account of Jacopa. It did smell a little down there, and was rather cold. The cold came from the stone floor, but also from the dead, I do think. The smell was from the chemicals that Jacopa and her fellows worked upon. The treated muslin that was put inside the dead in place of their organs, which would putrefy and cause us so many problems.

Jacopa was a marvel at her profession. She had a passion for it that, I think, offended other men and made them nervous of her, but I found her fascinating and it bothered me little that she chose such extinct companions. Only later did I realize how her work with those chemicals — the arsenic, you see — was causing Jacopa to ail. We spent all our lunchtimes together. We went together to see the puppets in the theater. Such life there, such battles among the strung people.

Paladins and Turks, they hacked each other apart — how we gasped at that. We did love the puppets, Jacopa and I. We were going to marry. But then, you see, the arsenic.

I come now, steady my heart, to Antonella. When I turn over the wood and try to summon her in paint, I start by placing the lozenge portrait of Jacopa nearby, for Jacopa and Antonella were sisters. Not twins, Antonella being the older by some two years, but there was definite family in their faces.

It was there that we met, at Jacopa's funeral, and both missing the same body we found that we had that body in common. We began to visit each other, then, because no other human being understood our grief as we did each other's. And there was Antonella, like her sister: a vision of her, only slightly older. We talked, and Jacopa was our great subject. Thus we kept her breathing some months after her death. We told each other tales, intimate tales of secret moments; we sculpted the very image of her out of words. Sometimes it was too painful a thing, as if we were opening the coffin and looking in, wounding each other with love. We kept calling her back, trying to make her solid, but increasingly, as the months went on, she grew dimmer. And we entwined ourselves around each other by the spell of our mourning until, not exactly knowing it, we had become knotted one to the other.

To show my gratitude and my sympathy, I carved a small goat for Antonella. I don't know why a goat and not some other creature; it was where the wood led me. I resolved to paint it in lapis lazuli — which is, I will entertain no arguments here, the most beautiful color of them all, and therefore expensive. How I miss that color. I had none of the magic hue myself, so I raised the cost of a small pot by selling a coat. (Which left me with one — what need had I for two coats?) Yes, I carved and blued the goat and gave it her. And that goat, dreadful beast, changed everything. She took it with trembling hands. Why such nerves, I wondered, 'tis only a goat! No, no, that was no everyday goat. Not to Antonella. Goat in hand, she grew tears and proceeded to weep upon the goat. She wept, as they say, uncontrollably. Such great heaving sobs! Such wailing, all caused by a goat. And then, ah, she fled. She fled me. All for a goat. What an unfortunate goat that was. For a time I most regretted that goat. I hadn't meant anything by it. Had I? What can the meaning of a goat be, other than *goat*? But that goat, I see it now, had meaning, I had meant something by it. It was a little blue messenger.

She came back, ten days afterward. No words then. We pulled each other's clothing off and tugged and held and loved every piece of each other with more longing and need than I had ever had before, or should ever after. What a needing, grasping, what a yearning, what afternoon beds, what flesh, what feeling. What need it was! And needs must.

Then, the breath recovered, head by head, length by length, come the words. They must: we came together by words and words were always around us.

She: We cannot.

I: No, no, we must not. For it is wrong, you do see?

But we did, again and more. And always after there was the guilt. The words curdling and ruining and the wrong of it all.

She: She is splitting us apart.

I: Let us not talk of *her*.

She: She's here with us! In this very room. She will always be with us!

Always there in our loving, the ghost. We

did trespass upon each other. And, over time, my Antonella, she could not do it. To her, it seemed the worst wrong. And the knowledge and pain wormed in her, it made her sick, until the bed was not the bed it had been before. And so then, she left. I could not find her — the first of my great searches, how my people do flee — and no one would tell me where to look. I never saw her again.

In distress I returned to the wood. I carved monsters then, for a period, monsters of land, monsters of sea, and painted them all with lampblack. And after, I burned them, every one. Antonella, I heard later, found work in a hospital as far away as she could, in Messina. And there, too early, she went out to walk with her sister. *Cholera morbus.* She was buried with the blue goat, I learned from a note sent by a Sister of Mercy who worked at the hospital. I could tell by the note that the sister did not like me and was unhappily following instructions.

I went home again back across the waves of the Strait of Messina. The long march up-country, back to the small town of my birth. They laughed to see me brought so low, such a sorry remainder of a porcelain empire. This spectacle: a scarecrow come home to Collodi. Goodbye, Antonella. Goodbye, my Nell. Goodbye, love.

5.

Should this journal be found and I not with it, I enclose here my likeness. This is I, for certain. Or, rather, I when last documented. I wonder how I differ now. I am not especially fond of this tintype but here it is, affixed on the page:

I leave this here for my son. I hope it shall find him: a blessing, a memento of his dear old abandoned father, a little proof. It was supposed to be taken to celebrate his first day of school, but as you will notice, the schoolchild is absent. But I must confess that I had another idea, behind this one: I was hoping the portrait

might be used to announce my creation — a little proof of my great work to send into the world before me, to attract the crowds. Collodi was long famous for nothing, but now, I thought, all the world should soon flock here to see my hand-carved son. That anyway was my hope when my thoughts went tintype.

It was taken at the shop of Master Paoli, he of the greatest of stores in all Collodi, where one might purchase anything from cheese to nails to schoolbooks to duck feathers and horsehair. In the back was Master Paoli's studio, where he took his (locally) famous photographs. And there, that day, was I. But as you see, the seat is empty. I had painted the backdrop, a commission from Master Paoli. It was a piece of artificial countryside and architecture, a trompe l'oeil: an eye lie. Having not yet been fully paid (some part of this payment was taken up in a schoolbook), I came to him sometime after my wooden-life went to school and he agreed to lend me his jacket for the occasion. As you can see, the jacket is made for a stouter man than I. I look worried, as my boy had not come home. I am looking away, anticipating his return.

And I own it: I was expecting not just a boy, but a fortune. I was wishing not just for family but also for fame. Do but consider that. How can one stomach such ingratitude? I blanch to think of it now. What fathering was that? How it shames me today. My past and present are not friends.

Some days I pray for him not to come, not to join me in this death. But come he shall, one day. I fear it so.

My son, I dream of you all nights. I search for you in my dark sleeping. My child, my pine nut, Pinocchio, how the thought of your living warms me now, all my doubts long banished. I smile, sometimes laugh, at the joy of it. Some scoff at pinewood; some will have mahogany, chestnut, rosewood, oak. But for me, please, only pine.

At times, I admit, I have become angry. At times I have lashed out at the wood around me. I have made me a little fire in fury. Once, in my fury, I even broke a bit of *Maria* off in my hand. Just a little. But now my fury and my *Maria* piece are gone with the ash.

But . . . to run away like that! To break away so surely.

Oh, my boy, keep running still — and be wary of the water. Oh, have you come to ground yet?

But to throw the child out to sea! My Pino set adrift, exiled from land, forbidden a home. I see him, I do see him lost on the great sheets of water. There's no one with him there. He is all alone with his terror. Smashed at by the waves. He needs not eat, my boy, but the salt water may do him such harm. Oh my boy, do not rot.

He cannot float forever.

Even wood wears out.

Keep up, my boy, however you can, keep yourself dry. The varnish! Yes the varnish will help you now. Don't be frightened. You shall find land.

One more word: Avoid any island that moves. For it is the shark, and it looks for you. Swim, swim away from it!

Are you, Pino, yet afloat? How terrible not to know. How monstrous to be so kept in the dark. Pinocchio!

I draw him now, lying out. Washed up. On land again. But I cannot tell by this drawing whether he is alive or dead. Which way does he fall?

There are but four candle crates left. I must be more sparing.

I have by now many pieces of broken chinaware that have come in with the post, little pottery crumbs of my fellow human creatures. I collect them all up, it is a pleasure with me. But today something new that

I have never known before. My host has lost a tooth!

I have found its tooth!

What victory this is.

How I do laugh at it, this monster's fang. What harm has this weapon done? What crushing? And now it is mine.

What must it have swallowed in its time, this creature?

A schooner.

A carpenter. That much is certain. And now its own tooth.

People, I suppose, with fake teeth in their heads, wooden or secondhand, must live in constant fear of swallowing a tooth. How often are milk teeth swallowed? I think it must be very frequent. Once, when I was a child, I swallowed a tin soldier. Down he went into me. Later he emerged again, but even after he was washed off, he seemed most changed by the experience. He looked, I thought, devastated.

What else, I wonder, have people swallowed that they ought never to have had within them? Fish bones? Chicken bones? Flies? Shells? Nails? Buttons? Pearls? Marbles? Dice? Small animals? Lead shot?

Do people with imitation teeth, I wonder, fear they are becoming a sculpture?

I shall scrimshaw this tooth. Scrimshaw:

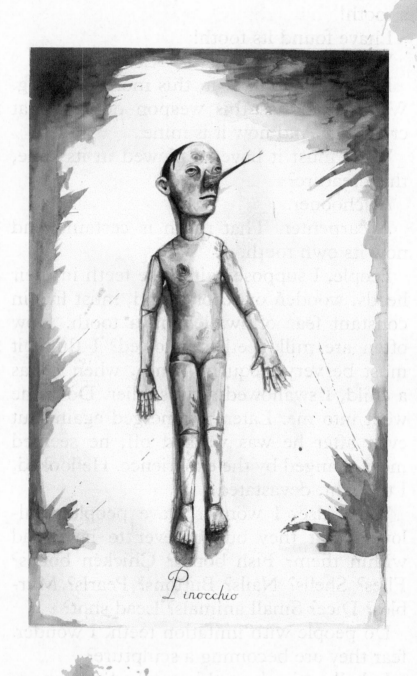

Pinocchio

might it be the most beautiful word in the whole language? Though it suggests too much time on one's hands. It is the occupation of the listless. Art comes from doldrums. Sailors with sharp points carve time on bone.

But what to carve? I thought at first of a whaling scene, depicting the creature being destroyed. I'd draw vengeance on its own bone. But now I think I should rather like to see some flowers here. I shall, with sharp point, drill cut flora upon it. To defeat the object that way, to change its purpose.

The darkness I know is one day closer, again.

I must take some pride — what pride I can — in myself.

And yet: First of all the losses, before I lost my father, long before my son, after Agnese and Sylvestra but before Jacopa and Antonella, I said goodbye to hair.

I am bald, I confess. There is no hair on the top of me. It ran away years ago. There is something very crude — something, why not say it, *lewd* — in the bald head of a human. The roundedness of it is at once comical and distressing. It is too intimate, it reveals too much, does the naked shiny topmost. As if I had my bare bottom on display. It makes a mockery of the dignity of the human species. It is a kind of autumn, when the head starts to lose its shelter. My autumn came early, in what should have been a longer summertime. Like a dog I found my hairs everywhere; I was shedding youth. I began daily to expose more and more of myself in public. My father before me had suffered from this disease, and no doubt blessed me with the same profound absence. But unlike my father — who allowed his naked pate to be always with him, a cannonball to youth, which by bowing down he pointed at people here and there — I decided as soon as the patch of skin was clearly growing, overtaking the land of my precious locks, that I must seek professional assistance. There was a shop I had in mind, it was Master Paoli's of course (a new business then, Paoli much younger), and I hurried to it. I entreated:

"Excuse me, please help. The garden atop me has gone barren."

"Come again?" Paoli's response.

"I wilt in the north."

"I'm sorry?"

"I have been abandoned, hairly."

"Make sense, can't you?"

"A wig, man, and quickly, too."

It was a little blond, I see that now. The children laughed at me, I see that now. "Cornhead," I was called, and no doubt deserved it. "Polendina," "Old Polly," "Yellow-Top." But I loved it, my yellow wigness. We went everywhere together. Before he left, my own son even took the wig for a moment and placed it upon his own head, then danced around the room. It did upset a little. But I kept it up. My wig and I were proud together. Even after the years, when my dear wig began to wilt — it is in the nature of things — and some of the wigmaker's rubber began to show a little, and so it looked, I suppose, less natural, still the lie was there to behold. Even so, I did not abandon my wig, we belonged together, you see, and had wearied similarly over seasons. As time stomps on we do lose things: hair one day, teeth the next. Eyes wear out, ears cannot hear, legs need rest, joints do creak as if they were turning to wood; and inside, the engine begins to shake. Nothing to be done. Natural enough, they say, but still it hurts.

That wig, so excellent a roof, I have lost. It is somewhere out in the ocean; after so long at home atop me; such loneliness it must feel. I wonder, does it seek companionship with the jellyfish? When I fell into the shark, perhaps understanding the terror, it chose rather not to go. So here I am, exposed of pate.

Something, in short, must be done.

Thus, over several days, I have kept a portion of sea-matter sealed in a tin box, where it has dried out at last and become a little like leather. I am, if nothing else, resourceful. From this I have fashioned me a new hairstyle, the height of fashion for today: a wig of finest seaweed. Here inside, I secure it with a dab of fish glue from my glue pot, and there it stays. Hallo! I feel young again, and ready should any visitor come upon me. Should my unlucky son appear at last, he will not find me underdressed.

I will keep this leviathan civilized. We are human, after all.

Sit up! Four legs to a chair! I shall not see your elbows!

Perhaps I may yet escape and save him.

Perhaps there is a way. Dig a tunnel? Find a hole? I shall think further on it.

Today, there being nothing marked in my calendar, I have set about the business of making myself a family. I have always been the sort that makes things, and I think I really must start again now, for if I do nothing but sit and groan in corners, then I shall go quite . . . *uncertain*. To keep the madness off, then, I shall make.

I was an only child. My mother, Iris, was

taken away by the Great Collector when I was but four years into the business of living. What did it? Why, dry cholera. The blue disease, the same that took Antonella, found Mama many years earlier. How blue she turned!

Afterward this left but me and him at home. Father, shut off and locked up in mind and body, few words, often a flared anger. Such a poor, hurt fellow; I understand that now.

But no, no! We'll start again. I shall magic me a populace.

It may take some time.

I did not eat much today. I had not the stomach.

I have with me here, in great supply, a quantity of hardtack, also called ship's biscuit. I am most fortunate in this companion and it does sustain me, though it gives me little excitement and has caused the loss of two of my teeth (small yellow peas not fit for the scrimshawing). At last, I find, we have come to an understanding: if I do not bite it, it allows me to keep my dents. Hardtack is best consumed with a great deal of liquid; the ideal method is breaking off a piece and sucking upon it, until slowly, with saliva, the hardtack gives up the ghost and becomes edible. It undergoes a great scientific meta-morphosis within the cave of a mouth.

I wonder if the same is true of me.

But hardtack, repast of the patient, monotony of the table, has, I have discovered it, another quality! It can only be described as another miracle.

One day (do not ask which, for Mondays here are identical to Fridays, Christmas like the summer solstice, Michaelmas, Candle-mas, and Martinmas all triplets), while I was chewing on some ship's biscuit, I found it of a sudden difficult to get air in me and I choked. I had indeed such a fit of splurt-ing and coughing, such a battle to find breathing, that I dislodged the offending half-mashed biscuit, catapulted the morsel from my mouth and sent it cannonading upon the captain's table. Panting but breath-ing, I staggered out of the chart room into the greater hollow to recover — leaving the expelled titbit, undisturbed, upon the land of desk. Forty-eight hours later, I spied the thing where it lay. In disgust I reached to hurl it from the cabin, when I found myself surprised by the touch of the thing. Hard-tack, when uneaten, is sharp but flakes eas-ily. Hardtack when eaten is a mush, a paste. But what I was holding now was something else. It was fully white, and hard as bone.

Ah!, I said to myself — for there is no further company — *the latest miracle.* I danced a little around the cabin. I kissed the wretched gobspat. This was a discovery of great import.

Why? What then did I have?

I had *clay* — something to sculpt with, a means of making things! True, I should have been happier with a quantity of wood, but there was only ship's wood for carving, and to pull the ship apart I must harm my home. But here was clay of a sort, and now my days could be occupied with a special purpose: I could make me a person out of clay. Clay child. A further remembrance of my lost boy. It was without any doubt that my fingers, moving in the air at the thought of clay, instinctively sought the shape of son. There was one slight concern: the more sculpture I made, the less food I had to eat. To eat or make? Full belly or empty head? I would rather starve, I told myself, if it meant I could craft one thing or another. So, then, make: create more and live a little less.

I ground a quantity of hardtack, dumped it into a barrel that proved watertight, and added some of the foul liquid that serves as carpet here. I mixed, swirling with greater happiness than I had felt in ages.

I did my mixing, the mush did its mush-ing, and I made me a head.

My boy. My boy slowly came out to me: life-size, palpable.

I could touch him.

Here, here you are. Is that you? Some-where, there? Yes, there he is, smiling at me, grinning, but sad, too, I think — a touch of doubt in the face.

Oh, boy, are you alive out there in the world? How terrible it is, the not knowing. Is he?

Do not come here. Do not tempt the great shark, for it is looking for you.

I think of him now, abroad in the world; is he still sea-tossed, or has he come alone on dry land? The crowds that must rush to him, the wooden life. The attention. All the clap-ping at his wonder. How he must bow for them. I see him clear. But me, what about me? It was I that made him. Do you ever tell them? Is that immortality, then — how the art is appreciated while the artist is gone? If so, then I say I hate it. To dark hell with it! I spit on it! What good can it do me? None. It gives me no feeling.

I'll have you home! I command you.

But no, *no*! I withdraw the command. Do not come here, my own!

I did it. Me alone. Ah.

Ah, yes, that face. I do know it, you see.

Sometimes I had to stop the frantic rush of creating him in hardtack, my hands shaking, my eyes too wet. Sometimes it was a little too much and I must run from it. It was then that I knew I had him. There in the clay. I made him as a flesh child again, for fear he may otherwise look dead. To be clear of the divide twixt death and life.

I gave him glass eyes. I stole them from the stuffed owl. It was a sodden beast anyway and no companion, it was daily hemorrhaging sawdust. And he did seem a little to live, then; there was a glint of life in the eyes. I would rather it was wood, of course — living wood. To think of him alive, to remember that first breath!

But there was to be no repetition, no, that was not its purpose, no little Horatio Hardtack, no Sebastien Shipbiscuit. This clay boy kept so still you'd think him dead. But he smiled at me, yes, even if there was a little mocking in it, yes. The purpose of such food-bust is memory, to keep memory alive.

Look there! There is a naughtiness in his face, is there not? Of course there is, he was no milksop, he was no corner child. There and here he is. You live! I made you! A likeness from my life, pulled out of the past and into solid biscuit.

Solid. Proof. Boy. *Pino.*

I should, yes, I should rather it were wood.

There is a stick here, too, a very good stick that came in with the post. Sticks are wood, after all, and I am susceptible to wood of any kind. I had put it on a shelf when it arrived, gazing at it as if it were Meissen porcelain, delftware, Whitby jet. The stick and I had known each other perhaps a week when suddenly I found its purpose.

Nose!

Yes, I have given the stick a name. Nose, it is called.

I like my bust well enough, though in honesty, hardtack is not the liveliest of materials. But wood! Yes, nothing better. I took my sculpture in hand and I gave my boy a nose of wood. *This much,* I said, *I can do for thee.*

How it sticks out! What a prominence!

A nose to match my boy's own long snout. A nose to honor, at last.

My hardtack boy looked so much better with the stick there, as if he were coming to life. Something like Daphne turning into tree, rushing into living wood.

I wondered for a moment if I should trim the stick a little, but I have not the heart. The memories. The saw. The switch.

I leave it be.

Finishing the bust of my child is another

little bereavement. I pat its cheeks. It is bitter, sweet.

Now that it's done, I find myself talking to it. Sometimes telling it off. Why did you pull my wig that day? Why did you kick? You are mine. Why, *why,* did you run away?

How dare you? How are you?

Come home. You'll not run away again, I'll see to it.

NO! NO! YOU MUST NOT!

6.

But three candle crates left.

I awoke in a rage, angry at my imprisonment, fearful that the beast might one day find my son. And that when it has us both in here, we shall all three drift down and perish at the bottom of the ocean. I must get out, warn him, ward him off. And I must do it this day.

Down I went, to the floor of the beast. From there I started clambering up the throat again, the pitch ever steeper, the road narrower. I fought the post coming in, slipped down, but was up again. I was doing well until a mean throatwave thumped me, smashed me back home again. Did I weep? No, never. I screamed in anger.

"YOU SHALL NOT HAVE HIM! I SHALL KILL YOU FIRST!"

I went at it then. There was a pick-like object in the *Maria*, and I commenced smashing into the floor of the beast. I'd tunnel my way out, as the best prisoners do. I'd dig my way to freedom.

I struck the surface with the pick. It did little, but a pinprick in its surface. And again. And again. The hole getting larger. More! A hole, finally! One I might sink my arm into. I was sweating then, in my fury; I meant there and then to dig my way out. With a candle alight on a crate beside me, I bailed out the blood that filled the hole, but the blood filled up so quickly that I could catch only the briefest glimpse of my endeavor. Still, there was no doubt, the hole was getting bigger. Joseph the giant killer!

I was in such a passion that at first I did not notice the shaking in the belly, the rumbling of the creature — until it *leapt*. A great heaving in answer to my tunneling, in pain I do suppose, and I leapt with it. It tossed me up into the air, the candle, too, and before I landed again the candle was out and all was dark and I lay in pain just as it swam in pain. And it was no good, no good at all. I held the Lucifer in my pocket, but it gave me such little relief.

The tunneling would never work.

I am so small.

I cannot kill it; it is not possible. The fish is too large.

My son, stay away.

■ ■ ■ ■

And yet, despite everything, there is life here! A crab, a tiny life in my beard. I call her Olivia.

Olivia gives me much comfort as she busies about my great landscape of hair, which is her home. I tap her very gently upon her flat head, as if she were my cat. And in return she flees sideways, or lifts up her dear arms and nips me. How it grins me to be so nipped. I am so proud of her. She is so brave, she makes me braver. She is excellent good company.

Such playing!

With the precise aim of being less frightened, I have resolved to stare the beast down. I have tried to ignore its existence altogether, but this — when it takes a deep plunge for example, or when it drips, stinks, creaks, gases, heaves, darkens, pinches, bites, and growls at me — I find impossible to sustain. And so I have wondered if, rather than feigning ignorance of the creature, I should do better to look it right in the face. It never shows itself — it cannot, after all, for I lodge deep within it — and so I must only guess what my prison looks like from the outside. Do prisoners, I wonder, consider the outward appearance of their gaol?

But, clever as I am, I have contrived an exercise.

I have painted its eye: Or, I should say,  what I suppose its eye to look like. It is a black eye, with some red and orange about it, and then thick hide all around. A small eye for such a big creature, but so dark that you might fall into it; a stomach of an eye, to be sure; a pit, a well, a cave, a death.

Every day, for ten minutes, I stare at the eye. (I say ten minutes, but it is only a guess. At least ten, I should say. Perhaps as many as thirty, though that is most troubling.) I sit me down in Captain Tugthus's chair, I place the beast eye before me, and I stare it down.

Sometimes — often, I should admit — the eye has the better of me and I tremble, but not for very long.

I tell it: You will not have my son.

Memento mori. Remember death. Ah, yes, I do not forget! Solemnly, every day, I prepare my rickety carcass. I, so to speak, pack my bags. I stare at my own exit. This way, I can say to myself: *Man, you man, you stared at that creature today!* I do impress myself. How brave! And so I feel better, and so I grow stronger. A knight fully armored, charging into war. A David staring down his Goliath.

Old age is a single room.

Ink. I am running out of you. And when the heavy bottle is out it will be another kind of death. I could write in my own blood, I suppose, but it wouldn't suit, and it would so limit my verbiage. I could write in its blood, the beast's, but how it would heave in protest. I have so little to luxuriate in, I would not run out of words. Oh, please, I beg, do keep me in words. Olivia, I fear very much to go silent.

7.

I dwell, some days, on the shape of my wooden child. The roundness of his skull, the curve of his spine. Yes, yes. The grain in his face like freckles on other children. The whole wooden constitution. The complete child. How the joints are. The fold of his knee. Elbows! His dips and bends and the harness of his little shoulders. Wooden clavicles. Wooden toes. The smell of him! Woodskin. Woodbones. Woodheart. Woodlife.

He cannot grow, my boy. (Except, of course, the nose.) Not like all the others. Wherever he is, he stays as he is; he is constant in his carving. (Unless of course the sea diminishes him.) He is not, may I say it, unlike those wooden men found in the holy houses upon their crosses. I have seen many such a wooden youth. In the Church of the Holy Spirit just by the river Arno in the city of Florence — I walked the twelve hours there in search of my son — I sat to rest in the chapel, and there before me, in my despair, was a young man made from a linden tree by Michelangelo Buonarroti Simoni when he too was young. So pure and sleek, oh, the gentleness of wood.

But even Michelangelo's boy, unlike mine, was made dead. His eyes are closed and he will never wake. But mine. How he kicked! Ha! Ha! He kicked!

Did I dream it? I sometimes wonder. But I cannot say. My head is not quite to be trusted. What is certain is that, last night, I carved again. But am I to be trusted?

I have been drinking. I have been at the wine. I tried it and found it went down very easy, and so one tin mug followed another, until a spirit grew inside me. It seemed to me like the very spirit of carving. There are ship's tools here, and the *Maria* is a wooden lady. I thought, I should carve again. But did I? Or was it only dreaming? I think I may have spent hours at the wood. And yet, if so, then where is my labor? Where the proof of my work?

Last night I think I made a child again. Oh, what a sin.

I pulled a portion of the *Maria* apart. I see where it came from. I woke up in the morning and found it gone, and gone it remains.

But such a face this time — a squished face, an ill-faced child. A wrong-faced boy. Not like the first, but a twisted idea of life. A shadow creature. A spleen child. Something from the deep, a dark, unhappy thing is what I made. It was the wine filling me with bad blood.

And then this thing I made, it scuttered, it spidered, it clicked on the floor.

It stuck its tongue out at me, a tongue black with wine.

A child made of unhappiness, a black bone child.

I carved him in the night, drunk and full of horrormood. I drunk-dreamed him up, this ghost of dark wood, this child of the *Maria* and me. And he moved!

Not the first son, but like the first son:

He kicked!

Like the first son:

He ran away!

Like the first son:

I have a bruise here where he struck.

But can I be certain? NO! I cannot. After all, parts of the *Maria* do tumble and disintegrate of their own accord. And I cannot fairly say I remember the carving, the making of the boy.

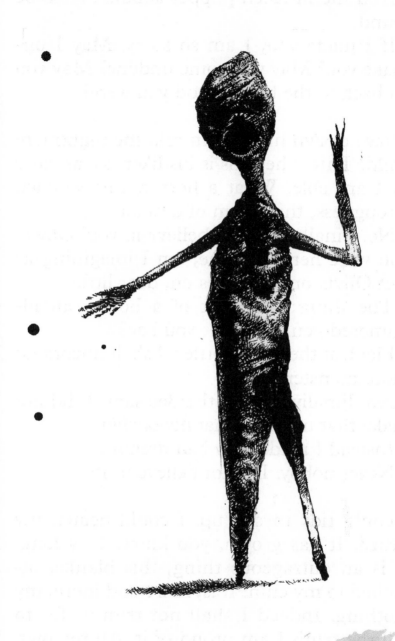

And the ill-faced puppet is nowhere to be found.

If I made you, I am so sorry. May I unmake you? May you come undone? May you go back to the black wood you were?

I have drawn him out in ink, the nightmare child: This is he, this is his likeness, as close as I am able. What a horror, this wooden wrongness, this totem of despair.

No. Finally I do not believe in you! Olivia, you were here. Tell me, am I imagining it? But Olivia only scuttles on, dear little.

The thing came out of a bottle, an ill-humored genie. I'll put you back.

I look at the wine bottles. I shall uncork no more monsters.

No. Finally, here is the decision: I did not make that unchild, that *nonocchio*.

Instead I made only bad dreams.

Never noboy. Do not believe in it.

I could tidy myself up. I could neaten my beard. It has grown, you know, very long. It is an outrageous thing, this blanket attached to my chin. It is, more and more, my clothing. Indeed I shall not trim it, for to tell the truth I am proud of it. All my own work, such growing! Perhaps, if I am ever to step upon anything but shark flesh, should

I ever have a different land, I might make a good living exhibiting my great bearding. Perhaps this is the longest beard in history? Perhaps there is my fortune! Imagine a town square, a man sat in the center with his beard coiled round and round, quite filling the place. I have tripped upon it often, and shut it in cupboard doors and snagged it all over the place, but I'll not part with it. It is after all Olivia's home. I like to lay it out and step back to better contemplate its lovely length, to see Olivia about her playground. How it makes me smile. It does me good. I have had bad dreams of it being gone. I have a terror of waking up clean-shaven.

And besides, how else can I tell how long I have been here if not by the hairs of my chinochin? It is an excellent timekeeper.

Beard clock.

Hair diary.

I have seen the ill-faced child again. In the dark. He's here when the candle stutters. When I blow out the candle, he comes in an instant. There in the darkness, the unhappy shadow. A cruel spirit — a wooden curse. I fear he means to hurt my boy.

Quickly, quickly! Hurry now! Something other.

■ ■ ■ ■

Oh! Tomato! I have just remembered you. Please forgive that it has taken so long. Tomato, lost to us now, I dedicate a little prayer to you. You would like a tomato, Olivia. I would share it.

Dear God, bless all the dear tomatoes. Dear God, in case you have forgotten, I'm down here in the belly. Dear God, I ate ripe tomatoes and they were so full of nature and the world. Dear God, return me, please, to the tomato places.

What can I grow here?

I have no sun. What may I grow?

Hair. I grow hair. Scarves of it.

Sometimes, in the night, I hear the ill-faced child breaking up the ship. Smashing it! Yet when I rush to the noise he is no longer there — and yet, sorrowful, the *Maria* groans. And comes to pieces.

I am being haunted. It is a spiteful wooden thing that haunts me.

Which shall go first, I wonder, mind or ink or candlelight or eyesight?

What helps me, most of all, is writing in this book. I must find something solid to do, something rigorous and time consuming, something true. Something honest.

There is a mirror here; it gets the news of my decaying. There I am. Still there. What sores and infections.

What, you again? I say when I see me. Hallo! I've seen you somewhere before, haven't we, Olivia?

In this theater there is only one actor (forgive me, Olivia) and the scenery never shifts, only ages.

Well, then, I suppose it is a piece of humanity. Aren't you? I whisper to my reflection. Do it then: A self-portrait. And let Olivia be the judge of it. To set beside the son.

Great artists, having themselves generally available, do portrait themselves. It is a familiar business. Done again and again, over many years, it is a thorough contemplation of time's bite.

I do it in hardtack, as a companion to the errant son, missing and so missed. I observe me and duplicate myself out of ship's biscuit. I make myself from my lunch. I build myself up. Come now, be smiling. But the smile keeps falling from the face. The hardtack droops down, it is honest stuff. It is too, too white, this new me. As I busied away, I had the sudden idea that I would decorate myself with some of the furnishings here about and thus add a little color, a little companionship, to my face. No medals, no, but rows of oyster and mussel shells for decoration. Eyes! My son has his glaring owl eyes, I should give myself eyes. My eyes, each time I look, are blue. And I have found, among my treasures, two blue pieces of sea glass, of such beautiful blueness, rounded and kissed and tumbled by the sea, tossed and played with until all the edges are curved out and can no more be danger. Sea: sandpaper. These I have made mine eyes. Oysters for ears are perfect. And a mussel for a nose, it has the bend of my snouting. And mussel shells, turned inside, to represent the hollows of my cheeks.

I have grown thinner since I came here, as who would not? Atop my head no crown of gold or thorns, but rather a coronet of seaweed. And for my beard a fine collection of rusted nails. (Some of these I have, with alarming ease, pulled from the *Maria*. With what troubling swiftness they have come out. My home! My home is rotten.) All these gifts given me by my gaoler. Yes, I have been most busy this morning!

That is I. Yes, yes, very like! Self-portrait bust with two oyster shells, three mussel shells, kelp, tinted glass, decayed nails. I stand back to admire it — and I start to shake. What do you think, Olivia? She scuttles away, hides deep within my beard.

It is not a pretty thing, that head there.

No, it is not. It is something beastly. Suddenly, I am terrified by it.

I find myself shrieking at it, howling.

A sea troll!

Monster of the deep. Am I, then, the monster? Do I nightmare myself?

I am recalled now of a certain artist. (Jacopa, it was, who told me of him.) A painter of little repute, from the land of Norway, a haunted place where ghosts are met on every street corner, in every wood. The painter lived out by some fjord on the edge of a deep forest, and there he painted, as his subject, great hulking trolls. Big grim faces, creatures as big as mountains. Many-headed, they were, clumsy and crude, eating children. Painters of drawing rooms and society asked why he painted such silliness, such fantastical subjects. He answered, at last: because they terrified him. He told them, I cannot paint a landscape without putting a troll in it. What you would call reality, what you see as truth and the everyday, doesn't interest me. Not for me the small fragilities of daily life, only the certain monster of death. Theodor Severin Kittelsen was his name. What a way to live, to paint trolls only. To fix on nightmares. Here, in the fish, I understand him better.

In truth, I am glad I have remembered him at all. Things I once knew, you see, come back to me only fitfully, at random. How to make mutton pie, for example; how many minutes for the perfect egg; my nine times table; which snakes have poison and which do not. Latin conjugations, verses from hymns, the Magnificat. And the man who painted trolls.

And here am I, and there am I, sea troll. Boo.

8.

Olivia has died. Oh, Olivia. I supposed she must, of course. She was so small and slight. I was always gentle with her. Even as I tsunami-rolled over in my sleep, I took care not to crush her. But delicate life, the clock-work is faulty. It is dangerous, Olivia, I kept telling her, to be so small. Do grow up, you! But she did not heed me. It is not her fault; I speak no crab. But I found her today, in a beard corner, still and blue. I tried to push her along a very little, but she scurried not. She had lost the knack.

She'll nip no more.

How I will miss the nipping of Olivia Crabb.

I keep her on the shelf, by the captain's pictures, by my drawing of my son. Dear, dead little friend.

I don't believe in you.
The ill-face has been back.
Sometimes he is here, right beside me,

the wooden thing, and when I reach out to touch him, he changes — there and then — into a door or bench or mast pillar, to some knob of wood. And yet, *I swear it,* the ill-face was just here.

Find your balance, Joseph. You are a man, a man inside a shark. Facts.

If you want better things than facts to ponder, make them up yourself.

I will tell a story, for I have no books to give me theirs. I will improvise a tale; it will go where it will go. To keep my mind from idling. To get me out of myself.

I will change the cast. A new child, not my son; not that wooden knot but someone else's. This new puzzle-fellow is most highly pleasing to me. He is pale, so pale; he is smooth and cool but chipped; he is a bit of something larger, but that bit has come to me.

He is part of a teacup.

Each time my monster host swallows some porcelain, I leap with joy. Why? Because it means we must be close to land — at least here is evidence of land! And what is in the ocean: water of course, fish, weed, some wood, but also something else: old bits of pottery. Broken pieces of china, shards that float, human daily life in fragments. This creature must have disturbed the bottom of some port, ingested what humans have thrown away. Like the great river Po that rushes through Turin and Piacenza and Ferrara, all the way from the Alps to the Adriatic, it carries with it small shards of human history, and when it floods it throws these pieces out on the burst banks: a little history of man in broken objects. So is it here with me.

Perhaps the world has ended, and these small pieces of shattered pottery are all that is left of *Homo sapiens*. Perhaps I am the last human, though I think myself dead sometimes. Yet even my dubious eyes spot the broken pieces that are thrown about by the busy ocean, until they float into the beast's mouth like seaweed. I clink two of them together, and it is a beauty noise!

What could be built from all this, the broken crockery of the seven seas? I have pieces from Ceylon, pieces from Haas & Čžjžek, pieces named Spode or marked *Doccia* or *Porzellanmanufaktur Gotha* or yet *Verbilki* — what mixing of the world. Not yet, however, one shard of my father's porcelain. Perhaps it shuns me. But these broken bits and pieces are, to me, great communications. I have plenty of glue, and so I have put the shards together — to make someone new. Will he live, I wonder?

I shall call you Otto, I tell him. Otto, because you are the same taken forward or backward; you are, like me, in a constant place.

Welcome, Otto. It seems to me that you were always meant to look this way — that you are not being constructed for the first time, but rather that I have put you back together properly at last. You have been decimated, poor Otto, but now, piece by piece, you are more and more yourself again. Slowly, you come to me. And I sit beside you of an afternoon, if indeed it is an afternoon, and do enjoy our time together.

What kind of a cousin are you, Otto? You always were, it seems to me, very fragile. You were born, much to your parents' distress, with very hard skin — so hard that you could knock upon it and it would give a clink. There was always something of the dinner service about you. Your nose, please do not be offended, always suggested a teacup. Your forehead, is it not strange, recalls to me the saucer. Your parents found it wise to keep you away from other children. You had a brother, do you recall? His name was Massimo, yes? And Massimo, as I have no need to remind you, was . . . *oversize.* Bigboned was he. Mimo, as he was affectionately called. Most heavy baby, enormous thing, mother heaving and cut, local doctor very proud. What a big clot it was! Biggest infant the town had ever seen, though it was a small town, of no historical importance. Even so, local celebrity. He was born, oh, loud Mimo, with all his milk teeth fully present. Oh, hungry Mimo! Oh, provincial monster! No herbivore this, no lettuce cruncher, no cucumber botherer. From the earliest age, it was ever meat with Mimo. How this fleshy flesh-eater ate! I do not think he could ever be fully satisfied but needed more — not just meat, but love, too. He was hungry for everything. Your parents gave him everything they could. Who can blame them for feeding Mimo with so much love? And there he always was, with open arms, hugging and kissing and smothering, always wanting more . . . until the parents grew tired of it. They loved their Mimo, but so much affection, so much need, can become a tiresome thing. They needed some other little pot in which to keep a part of their love.

So then, after a troublesome confinement, one weeping day, you, my dear, delicate Otto, were born.

Otto did not cry when he came into this world of cups and saucers; indeed he clinked. He was shiny and white, with blue words on his ears that read ROYAL

DALTON, STAFFORDSHIRE EN-
GLAND, BY APPOINTMENT. That was
his birthmark. How proud his parents
were! They saw instantly that he belonged
on the mantelpiece and put him there.
How smart he looked. The neighbors came
in their Sunday clothes to look upon Otto
of the mantelshelf. Some were jealous, but
they tried to hide it.

"What a lovely piece," they said. "How
well it shows off the room."

"Ah, yes," said a shiny neighbor who was
certainly better than anyone else she had
ever met. "I have a great aunt who produced
a spectacular child with Meissen. A wonderful child that was, always destined for
great things. She was sent to palaces, and
was even used by Catherine the Great. She
had the most beautiful skin I have ever seen.
All went well with her until, alas, she was
dropped by a servant. She leaked in old age
and no one could stop the leaking. Poor In-
grid. Such skin."

Otto kept still upon the mantelpiece. He
never cried, good child that he was. When
he was old enough, Otto asked about going
to school, but his parents considered him
too precious. His laugh was a most satisfy-
ing sound that never went on too long, like
the noise of a lid being put on a teapot — it

fitted him exactly. His mother dusted him often, and he shined up beautifully.

After Otto was put on the mantelpiece, Mimo was denied the front room. You are too clumsy, they told him; we fear he will break. Mimo would pound about outside, until Otto jogged a little on his shelf. "Otto! Here I am!" his brother cried. "Come and play with me, or at least just let me in! Why do you not talk to me. Otto! Otto!" His parents hugged their big hungry child less and less, and they left him on his own a great deal. Over time he wandered from the house and found friends among the unemployed souls who gathered near the town's workhouse; those washed-up people took a pleasure in Mimo, who spent his afternoons doing odd jobs in the workhouse, showing off his strength. When a worker there would scream and bellow and break things — which was not uncommon, for the place was unrelenting and wore the workers down — Mimo was directed to take hold of the unhappy person and clamp them within his arms until at last their weeping or screaming ceased. Mimo was so good at hugging people into silence that once or twice some ribs were broken, but nobody minded very much because a riot had been averted.

Most of all, though, Mimo longed to hug his brother. Sometimes he stood outside the front room looking through the windows, until they kept the curtains drawn. Once, tapping on the window to attract his brother's attention, he smashed the glass altogether; this caused Otto to give out a loud, high wail, something like that of a kettle — and how his parents fretted over their endangered child! Picking up the shards of glass, they imagined themselves picking up pieces of Otto and they wept. Mimo, it was decided, should stay in the workhouse, where he was so useful and the work suited him so well. They visited sometimes, but not often, and less so with time.

From the window in the front room, Otto could see the bell tower of the town church. It gave him great ideas of height, the tower did, and might perhaps be to blame for the strange growing upward that occurred in him around his thirteenth year. Soon he was too big for the mantelpiece, until his parents were obliged to move him to a cast-iron end table. He started growing small handles here and there about him, no matter how much his mother discouraged it. A new spout was found on him. He began to smell faintly of the sea.

"If I were you," said the neighbor with the

Meissen antecedent, "I would put him in the attic."

It was the nicest room in the house, the front room, with its carriage clock (Otto's favorite companion when he was small) and its empire sofa (which, though uncomfortable, improved everyone's posture). But Otto no longer fitted; he had outgrown such elegant things. The mother and father, exhausted, agreed that it was time — for the empire sofa and the carriage clock were likewise most fatigued — and Otto was taken up to the attic.

But Mimo was around so seldom that no one remembered to warn him away from his brother's new home.

. . .

Ha! What nonsense! Enough, at least, for now.

9.

I want and fear the creature's death. I mean my fish-house. How long may it live, and how long has it lived already? A thing cannot go on indefinitely. All life must end; there are rules that say so. Everything wears out. Shall I go first? That would be for the best.

Should my indifferent host predecease me, should that habitual thud of its heart muscle stop and horror silence flood in, what then should be my fortune? There would be a going down, a horrible final descent to the bottom of it all, the loneliest place that ever was: five hundred thousand thousand leagues under the sea. There, in a darkness that makes my daily darkness a midday brightness, my home would rot and rot and daily shrink about me. No post would come for me, and my address would slowly cease to be. Of course homes do slowly collapse everywhere on earth, you should not get too attached to them, that is true. But my home is alive, and if it dies I shall perish, too.

And then my son shall at last be safe.

But two crates left.

A requiem for Olivia Crabb.

Olivia's old pelt is decaying on me. She is not nearly as much Olivia as she has been. Every day she turns into a caricature of herself. I do what I can. Soon she will have nothing in common with Olivia at all.

I have painted a small portrait of her on a clamshell. "For Olivia," I cried at the shell. I painted her there with quiet dignity.

Olivia, alive; as you were in the best of days. What a nipper you were. I do not forget.

I have thrown away the rest. I do not care for it anymore.

I have made a likeness in candle wax. It is a small personality, trying to say something. It sits quite well atop some wood I dislodged from the galley ceiling.

I have made fires from bits of the *Maria* to save on candles; I have axed her here and there to get a little warmth. But each fire for me disturbs the shark some, and each means I have less home. And this home, the *Maria,* is missing more and more, and if I take too much, then all may collapse and be home no more.

My mind returns, though, to Otto. So: A bedtime story, of the kind I used to tell the wooden boy in the wooden bed. (No, I never, I only wish now that I had.) Listen then, dear boy, and help me with your good attention as I make amends.

By the time Otto had been moved to the attic, Mimo had grown into a young man. He was very big, the biggest in the town. He rarely went home anymore, but when he did call at home he always broke something — a vase, a bell jar, a terra-cotta bust. He had free roam of the house, his parents lacking the nerves to follow him, and always there was a little breakage and the house shook and then again with brief waves he was invited out again.

You will recall Otto, last we saw him, was living in the attic. Well, here is the problem. Suddenly, as they were sitting together in the front room, the parents felt a sharp wind hurtling at their bodies, and this wind was called Regret and it was also called Loneliness. The room had never felt quite right without Otto in it, as if it were missing an essential piece of furniture. How naked was the mantelpiece, how dolorous the end table. And then, you see, the biting wind.

There was a gagging in both parents, a simultaneous guttural groan. And this was the noise out of both of their throats:

"Ot!"

For Ot, Otty, Ottil, Ottifer, Ottibald they had called him, back when they dandled, and Ot now was the sound of their pain. Ot! they cried, like bellowing bovines in panic over their calf. And in concert did they ascend the stairs and knock upon the attic door. That door, which kept Ot out, was now opened to let Ot back in. But the parents could find no Ot in the attic, or in the house, or anywhere else, to be dusted and mantlepieced.

"I have not hugged my brother!" said massive Mimo. But no one had mentioned hugging, so why had he? And why was his face so red?

All around the town the parents went, hearing everywhere the sound of pottery breaking; the deaths of tureens and vases and jugs and mugs. They walked and fretted till they looked like broken receptacles themselves.

Police came and searched. They searched everywhere in town, every cupboard, kitchen, corner and understairs, attic and cellar, and in the rush they upset things, and here and there were breakages. But amid all that shattered crockery, not a single piece had been the milky flesh of Otto the Lost.

Suspecting that Mimo in all his great clumsiness was to blame, the people who ran the workhouse began to employ him less and less. There was an outbreak of theft, and this, too, was blamed upon Mimo. And so, in the end, out of love and loss and in the spirit of adventures that are found in books and not in life, Mimo, Massimo, set out to hold the world on his own. He was never seen in the town again. At length his parents forgave him and looked for him at the workhouse, but he was not there. So they sat in their house, childless again, and talked of children. And every time they drank tea, each time they sat before a plate, they missed Otto with sharp pains. Until the very thought of cups and plates and food made them ill, and they ate less and ever less, until they were dead.

10.

What fish there are to fish! I'll list me a list, a fish list. Listen, fish, I call you all. I call you drum and loach, I call you lamprey and smelt, I do not forget pomfret or turbot, halibut, pike, trout. Eel, bass, chub, cod, carp. Mackerel and dory and blowfish and blackfish and whitefish. Bream and brill! Gar and barb and goby. And what, fish, are you made of? Of other things: catfish, dogfish, boarfish, mudfish, ponyfish, swordfish, tigerfish, elephantfish, frogfish, goatfish, trumpetfish, rainbowfish, rockfish, boxfish, hagfish, jawfish, handfish, bonefish, and lungfish.

Sole!

Flounder!

The ill-faced one has been moving my things! Twice he has hidden Tugthus's log. I have found it at last — and not where I left it.

Next, I fear it shall take the tinderboxes away.

Ill-face is upon me!

Here I am?
Who wrote this?
I did not write
this.
I did.
Where
are you?
Everywhere.
Are you true?
You waste the page! I shall
run out of pages. Get off my paper!
Stain! I'll have no more white.
Help! Who shall help?
Help!
Mama. I look for help to my mama. I have made her, here, in good ship's biscuit. A hint of blue about her, she looks in pain but very beautiful. Is that how she was? I can't be sure. She seems to me a little Virgin-like. I have given her hair from some fishing net that came in with the post. I think it quite fetching.

I am so happy to have her here, though her face is slipping. Mother, the blue lady. It is something like love.

Better. I am better now.

I have no more ship's biscuit.

I have opened the final candle crate.

There is no neat plot to a man's life. There are endless days, which are as like as twins. Mornings and afternoons and nights, one after the other, no true escape but only the calendar to show that the day is gone, and here comes another to take its place. The changes, when they come, are mostly gradual. Weather changes the scenery, yes it does — but not here. Here all is constant. Sometimes, true, there is a sudden movement, a genuine swift progress and then there is violent change, but then the slowness comes back again.

Of late a strange blackness is come upon the *Maria,* as if she is burnt. I think, surely, this must just be the blackness of the stomach I live in, nothing more. But it seems to me very like a spreading burning, and I have begun to wonder if it is the work of the ill-face. This blackness is not yet in the cabin, so I sit here, where I can ignore it well and think on other things.

When my father died, it was suddenly. His heart was done with him; it was exhausted, the poor old muscle-pump, and refused to go on, like a conductor walking out, and all the instruments quitting in his wake. Such a dear thing, life. Suddenly no movement. What was alive and moving changes its color and loses all assertion; it retreats and becomes mere matter. It grays so quickly, I have seen it. There he was. Father on the floor, then Father no longer, something other instead: a sculpture of Father. But Father himself had left the scene.

"Babbo!" I screamed.

No answer.

"Babbo," I whispered.

How to get him comfortable afterward? Tidy him up. There now.

Babbo. And so I must go on, fatherless. It has happened before; it was always going to happen. Still, it hurts.

The business, as I've said, was in ruins. Great debts, it was discovered, and in the drawers and in the ledgers a broken business was found. Was it my doing that broke all the plates? I was heir to nothing very much, and so there was nothing to keep me from giving in to woodwork. I left Collodi. An itinerant carpenter or else the workhouse. And then, along the way, so carefully did I work upon wood that, in my great urge to become a great someone, I became a father myself. And there again, the pain, the joy.

Give me one minute more with my son, just one minute more, and then I'll close my eyes and keep them shut. Oh, but he must not come. Shark, have you forgot?

Suddenly it came to me: the answer might be found in the shark's stomach.

I took a wooden club from the *Maria* and hastened down onto the sharkfloor. There it was, thrashing in the thin water.

An octopod. Flinger of ink. Writer of darkness. I killed it.

I slapped it hard against the *Maria* just to make sure. Even so there was modest movement. But then it stopped.

I said a brief prayer.

Then, looking at what I'd done, I picked up the body and laid it down on the captain's table. I pulled the head and the tentacles out of the body cavity. The other innards came, too, as if they were curious. In the gutting I found the creature's ink sac, small and silverish. There are two sacs to every squid: the main one, in the body, and a smaller sac behind the eyes. I held them up before the captain's ink bottle and cut. The ink slugged out.

Here is ink enough. I'm not done with writing yet. I have ink enough!

And yet, after I slept, I woke and saw it: the ill-face had been here again. There's black shadow in the room, which I am certain was not here before.

Not just the squid, then. Darkness, down here, from without and within.

He'll not hurt Tugthus and his card-backed people, I thought. I'll see to that. What noise he makes, though! How the *Maria* calls out in her distress.

I do not know very much of Captain Tugthus, but I have some of his small possessions, for now they are mine. One day I should like very much to return them to him, but I do not dwell on that. What I do find myself preoccupied by, now I keep more and more to his rooms, is precisely Harald Tugthus himself, who he was, who he is. This I cannot answer, for he does not stand forward, though I call to him often enough. He left no picture of himself. But I have proof of his exact dimensions in the clothes he has left me. Captain Tugthus still has his trousers here, and his jacket. I have shirts of Tugthus. I know what undergarments touched the limbs and parts of Tugthus. But do I then know the shape of Tugthus?

How the ship calls out; it is never silent now. The snaps, the groans, such arguments amongst the wood. And the blackness — the blackness is spreading sure.

Oh, being more and more inside the captain's two rooms, I have found a hair of Tugthus! What could be more precious? I squint at it in my brave candlelight and I ask it: Please, please, give me something more! Give me knowledge! What is it I demand? Only this: Tell me, please, the color of Tugthus's hair. Was he dark or fair, perhaps already graying; had time stamped him? Did he curl up top, I wonder. Were you disorderly, or did you part? You did not crop, and I am so pleased by that, for you are no felon, Harald.

So, with hair held tight between right thumb and forefinger, I approach the flame — not too close, for hair does love the flame and will perish by it in an odorous instant. So then, reveal yourself!

It is red!

Oh, Tugthus, you are a ginger nut!

Somehow I have always known it. For you, you see, are like as a candle to me. I warm myself by your fire. Hearth Harald.

This makes you pale, sir.

Freckled? Perhaps. Or have you, over time, lost those little dots of joy, of youth? Your eyes, then, a bright blue? No, green I should say. I am coming to know you now. I see your hat — it has known the exactitude of your headtop, it has covered up red like a candle-snuffer. Yes, yes, I know you better now.

Where shall I place this sacred line of red? I shall trap it within glass, in a bottle from the medical chest. I tied the hair to a weight and let it drop in there, safe now, perfectly imprisoned. There it is, held beneath a stopper, in my museum.

Exhibit
A hair of a redheaded human (Capt. H. Tugthus)

Here I place a collection of your things —
the whole costume, all the outer covers, even
without the main creature within. With this
red hair, with the small toothmarks around
your pen, with the bottle of schnapps you
left me half-finished (now fully gone), with
the curves of your handwriting — I think
that I am ready.

Come, Tugthus! I summon you. Captain
Harald, let me know you. I have the hair;
I have the clothes; come fill in the great
blank, the desired unknown. Here, come
here with paint, come here on wood. Don't
be shy, not to me.

I wrenched a panel, a little *Maria,* from the chart room wall, and made him:

And he is not my only company. I have, too, this woman living here with me.

And I will place her here, in the book, for good keeping.

Of all the possible faces I might not perhaps have chosen this one, but here she is. She is very faded, poor lady. I wonder if she is still living; I do hope so, but there is something about her that says perhaps not. She seems to be fading away, though her presence is keenly felt. She is a strict dame, of that there can be no doubt. And I like her for her strictness, for she says to me, in her peevish glare: Come, sir, do make the most of it, shall you?

This woman, I can see, knows her Bible excellent well. She may not be a deliverer of humor. I suspect she spends her life at scowl, and that the scowl, after long rehearsal, has made a permanent home upon her face. She has also, I do wonder, a certain care for pastry, as she does lean a little toward stoutness. Black is her favorite color, though I cannot tell what she is mourning. She is not my woman, but she is a sensible presence here. I think even the ill-face is a little scared of her.

Her name? Yes! Of course. It is Mrs. Tugthus. How old they were when they met, I do wonder, and when they first loved. When I think of her as the captain's wife I am filled with a great tenderness toward her. She keeps her house very tidy — physiognomy instructs me in this — and she inspires me to it as well. If she commands a thing, then it must be so.

We do share her a little, Harald and I.

I see her in the streets of Copenhagen; I have never been there myself, but her foreign face brings a little of the city to me, and now I am an international!

Proper lady. Good lady. Your eyes the lightest blue. Strict lady. My lady of the shelf. This faded image was held and regarded many a time by Harald. Her image, on the card, is so weak that I fear it might desert me. Was it the intensity of Harald's gaze that made her so faint? I should miss her terribly should she fade altogether. In her quiet conviction, she gives me hope. Don't go, please don't go.

Dear lady, thank you for your patience and for your sternness, for I do need some shaking up. You give me courage.

You see how Harald looks after me? Here is Harald's other picture, two of two. Here is a younger lady, not fading like the Mrs T. but clear upon the card. How determined the face, but I have found in study, a little uncertainty in the eyes. Does she lack

Harald's other photograph,
here inserted

confidence? I do like her clothes. This young woman is very well cared for. She must be, I think, the daughter. Oh happy Harald, to have such a child in your life. For truth, Miss Tugthus looks to me an excellent daughter, dutiful and fond and good. One who would never run away. And what thorough clothing does she wear, what care in dress. What buttons are these!

I am most privileged to have these two in my life, in the chart room and the cabin, in the belly with me. They give me much strength. Miss Tugthus looks away from me, out to her future, which I hope is full of love. I think it will be, I have every confidence in her future. But it is Mrs. Tugthus who is kinder, to my mind, for she looks straight at me and in her attention there is communication.

It is dialogue, you see, twixt her and me.

A great splot of ink. Where did that come from? It wasn't here a moment ago. It will not wipe off. I do not love it. How came it here?

11.

I had no notion upon waking that this day should be so extraordinary. But so it is. I have fresh company in my life! Such new-ness today. I am so grateful.

Let me tell you straight: there is a boy living at the back of a drawer in the chart room. I found him only by pulling the drawer out the entire way. He has been here all along, but he kept himself so quiet I did not hear him. Today, though, being so much in the captain's room, among the captain's property, I found him out! This new life!

What a shock it is, after all this time to see another face.

I found him just this morning (I call it morning, you'll not mind that), in the top drawer of the captain's desk, way at the back underneath everything. Otherwise I'd have known him sooner. Another picture! Another face. I think it must be that Tugthus

has a son! But why, son of Tugthus, are you kept in the drawer?

Did you perhaps disappoint? Did you disobey? Did you run away, recreant? You do look a little difficult. Did it hurt very much, the fall toward adulthood? Never mind! I stand by you, whatever your crimes.

Does the shark own my art, or do I?

But forty candles left.

There are hooks in the main cabin, for lanthorns perhaps, for fish business. I have seen them there. They hold fast and seem strong. I have been wondering over them for some time now. Earlier this day (or this night; again you'll forgive me) I pulled a bench up close to one. I hooked my clothes around the back of my neck, over the hook, until I was confident the hook had a good grasp. Then I kicked the stool away. I hung there. Upon the hook. My feet inches from the ground.

I was suspended. I was a prisoner of the hook. I kicked the wall, I made dents, but the hook would not let me go.

Help! Help!

What, I thought, should happen if ill-face finds me here?

I could not get down. Struggle as I might,

I was a prisoner of the hook. What started as an experiment became a torture.

I hung as if I were a coat. Some mere thing and not the person I know myself to be. An outrage, to be so imprisoned. I was a thing myself!

Pity, pity the things.

I know not how long I struggled, dangling there, until at last my rotten clothing gave way and I dropped painfully to the floor.

I scrambled back to the captain's rooms before the ill-face could find me. Such horrors in my head. Such thoughts.

I'll tell you something straight: I have grown a very great hatred of hooks.

I think I will, I think I may, Captain Tugthus, give words to your life. For the story of your fate has come to me, in a dream. I saw him, the ruddy captain, upon mountainous waves, climbing high and falling low, clinging to a dislodged piece of *Maria* that came from the main vessel as the great fish attacked her. About his length it was, this wood, and width, too, like a dancing partner. Tugthus was separated from his crew; they were surely clambered thick upon a dinghy and made it safe to land. Not so the captain, for he was the sea's plaything. He was thrown and lapped and chewed upon, but he did not let go of his *Maria* piece. Not him. For weeks he was sent this way and that, back and forth, upward and down, his brain beaten, his body withered. But in his head, still there, was Harald Tugthus: Captain.

His thoughts were all Denmark, and daughter and wife — son, too, though perhaps less so, or perhaps sometimes more. He saw them, his family, in the deeps below, waving at him. In the long bobbing nights the ghosts came, but he did not let go. In time, he grew so waterlogged that the only tight-warm place was deep in his skull, which his piece of *Maria* kept dry above the endless drink. What things he saw while floating, all his life sailing by. He never called out, nor ever despaired. On and on, there and there, now storming, now calming, a red beacon adrift. I cannot speak for all the greens of his misery, I cannot name you his blues or his grays. Blacks I can do, those I know. But seaweed though he had nearly become, the flame of his hair was still burning bright when at last did he, Captain Harald, cease his traveling.

He was washed ashore, barely breathing, not far from Cádiz, having been pushed there by all the dead of Trafalgar. It was said he was more fish than man by then, that in parts his skin had grown scales and his eyes were become fish eyes. Such tales are told of seafaring folk, of course, and not all are to be credited. All I know for certain is that they never could separate him from his piece of *Maria,* even after he was returned to his home and wife.

He had grown, in his time afloat, highly sensitive, the captain had. Whenever they ran him a bath, he wept. Even the sight of someone blowing into a steaming cup of broth, creating that limited whirlpool, unnerved him. He never did go down to the docks again. But he ate fish, still, and with gusto — *only* fish, in fact, and preferred it uncooked.

Whether Captain Tugthus ever allowed his son home, I cannot say.

My thoughts are all of freedom now.

But he has gone home, Tugthus. I do report it.

He is at home. His hair is grayer now, but a hint of red still remains.

12.

I am here!
  Ill-face is come back! I have lit candles.
  More light!
  More light!

13.

After so long, I have made a fire again. What a flaming! What a light it causes.

It started with some thickness of wood I pulled away from the *Maria*. I had the need to whittle, I had a necessity for carving, and with Harald's jackknife (which is none too sharp) I went about it for perhaps three hours, turning the wood round and round, inspecting it closely at times, at others from a distance, that I might know it well and judge it truly.

It is hard for me to explain the small ecstasy of woodworking: the gouging, the chiseling, the shape coming; O joy of hunching over and turning the wood into something other. I do accomplish this metamorphosis. Perhaps I am a genius, after all, and — here is the pain of my glory — no others but I are aware of it.

I took that shipwood and carved a flame. The flame atop a torch, a beacon flower, a great warmth. A beautiful flame that, to my eyes, did truly seem to flicker and curve. I made movement out of lump. I carved a fire and it warmed me, as the exertion heated my muscles, even caused me to sweat a little.

True, my flame gives off no real heat. But it shall last longer than any fire. It is the illusion of flame, and that illusion is worth more to me than any real inferno. It is an *idea,* you see, my portable wooden warming. Sometimes I am sure I hear it crackle and spit! This one log might last me a thousand years.

Does it warm, in truth? No, no, I am still cold. I think I shall never be warm again. But I huddle me now, around my wooden fire, as if it were my child's wooden heart,

and I find some moments' peace.

Did I hurt my boy, I wonder now. With the screw eye — did it pinch? And that hook, I wonder? I shall sit me now, around my fire, and stare into the flaming like an old whaler contemplating his extinguished seas.

The *Maria,* there can be no doubt, she is coming apart.

The ill-face has taken the forecastle and the wheelhouse. I fear to go out to that part. It is all black and charred. There's no life in *Maria,* not that part. It has grown strange black roots — lying branches, snakes of rot and disease. And all black. The black, it is spreading. It is sprawling, twisting. The darkness is ever creeping.

Laura. The last in my inventory of women. I must now write down Laura.

(Am I truly to count Laura as one of the loves of my life? I think I might. I lay down the suggestion here, but I place it in parenthesis. It is for the reader to decide. I have told no one of her before, and write it down now with considerable anxiety.

I fear so much the telling of Laura. She seemed to me so very true, so absolutely real . . .

166

No, no, I do go about it in the wrong way. Let me explain.

Back when I had a little home, a room, gas was introduced to our town. It was the business of the town mayor, Alberto Crespi his name: the undertaker's son, who once spied me with Agnese and told on us. Now this boy, grown to mayor, strove to make the town modern. He wished to boast of his own modernity — Collodi stumbling into the nineteenth century — and my room, being a portion of the town almshouse, was under his jurisdiction. If I did not keep up with my rent, my next falling should be the workhouse.

At Crespi's direction, pipes were put in. Wall sconces — nothing elaborate, mind, but the cheapest available. I turned the tap and there came the smell and then the blue flame. Mostly I continued to candle-light my nights, but still it was there. I could hear it at times, very quietly, whispering. A little shushing it was, suggesting I might like to take a little nap. Sssh, sssh, it went. Sometimes I had headaches. They were new to me, these growing poundings upon my skull.

I had been with the gas perhaps the whole of a month when, one dull morning, there she was sitting on the end of my bed: Laura. She had a neat black dress with a white lace collar. She wore sensible black shoes, like a governess. She sat very upright. Her hair had a central parting. Her lips were slightly blue, but there was an overall greenness about her, as if she were not completely well. Her eyes were larger than any other eyes I have seen in a human head.

She was there. So clear. But if I moved very close she was gone from me.

When they came to our street — my neighbor had reported a problem and they checked all the houses — they inspected mine with too much proficiency. They caught the whispering and they suffocated it. They murdered it.

Laura, my dear Laura — I named her so myself — was a gas leak. She was all methylethylene.

After they sealed off the gas, there was never more Laura anywhere.

I called out for her, sat by the places she used to sit. How I missed her! Even if she was slowly poisoning me, what a beautiful, what a heartbreaking poison she was.

Laura, who never really lived, and yet I was in love.

Sometimes, lately, I fancy I see her here inside the fish, always just a little too far away for certainty, just out of grasp, just out of candlelight. Laura on the forecastle deck. Laura in the messroom, rocking back and forth, sitting in the black. Laura at the foot of my bed. Laura deep within the belly of the shark. Laura whispering and shushing. With the ill-face.

After Laura left me, so alone in my days, mourning her, I decided I must find some more solid companion, that it was indeed not good for me to remain alone. I thought of the puppets I had seen in Palermo, I wanted something astounding like that. I needed some other human form in my little room. And so it was that I called upon my friend Cherry, with whom I'd been at school all those years ago, he who gave the teacher so much trouble, he who now has five rooms to himself. [His real name is Antonio, but they call him Cherry on account of his entirely red nose — the drink, you see.] I asked him if I might have some wood, for I longed to make a person, a companion, a fellow traveler. A jointed child that could dance and fence and make great impossible leaps. And who might also earn me my living, for the workhouse had never felt closer.

It was then, when I was least expecting it, that I summoned life.)

The blackness has come down the captain's corridor. Ill-face is taking over. A black root under the door.

"Come, come now."

Thank you, Mrs. Tugthus.

And what became of Otto, do we think? I think I know now. I have the ending.

Let us quickly pull back time again, to the moment when he was still there, in the highest regions of his parents' homestead. Up in the attic, from the window, Otto saw different things from before, when he lived at ground level. From that height there was a good view of the harbor and the boats and all the fish business. And he loved to look there and longed to be out there with them, but feared to go downstairs and out the door. He had never once been outside, not in all his life; his parents would never allow it. They were hard people, you see, intractable.

One day, his brother came to the highest door. "Otto! Otto, let me in."

"Who is there?"

"Massimo, your loving brother. Let me in."

So he did! And it was a weeping reunion.

Otto hugged his brother hard; there was the sound of a crack, but no sign of it upon him though they searched, and certainly nothing had fallen. How much good it did them, to see each other then. Afterward, Mimo would come often, he would go upstairs to the attic and always there was a crack, but not yet more than that.

"I want to go out," Otto said. "They will not let me, but I want to go."

"Come down the stairs with me now. We'll go out together." Mimo was employed as a dockworker by then. He had the run of the harbor, and he longed to show it to his brother.

"They shall never allow it."

"Defy them!"

"It would break me. I could never do such a thing. I try always to be a good boy. It is not in my nature. I would come apart."

So he stayed in the attic, looking out the window at all the ships from all over the world. Until, at last, after so many seasons, he could bear it no longer. When Mimo next came — "Otto! Otto, let me in" — he let him in as usual, only this time he said:

"Hug me, Mimo. Hard."

Again the cracking, but louder this time. (How the *Maria* does crack as I write this! It crackles and spits as if it were aflame, until

171

I am scared to go out. I have heard ill-face creak just the other side of this door.)

"Hug me, Mimo, until I shatter. Then take me far from here. Scatter me and show me all the world. Let me go free. Hug me, Mimo, very hard."

When Mimo did, there was a small explosion, and his brother fell to bits.

Mimo was devastated at what he had done, though it had been his brother's command. In mourning, he began to distribute the pieces of his brother among all the ships in the harbor. He contrived to stow each shard secretly away, to hide them on board as he carried in the cargo. Days later, those ships all sailed off for the distant lands of the world. And so off went Otto, severally, to Tasmania and Ceylon and the Cape Verde Islands and Saint Helena, to Nootka Sound and the Barents Sea and to Cape Town and Cape Horn and the Lizard and the Arctic and the Bosporus and the Aegean. And though he had blown all over the world, I, that am an old man hidden inside a shark, was able to collect him when everyone else had forgotten. He came to me, in pieces, and I made him whole. My very best work. Save the one.

I have put in the last piece. Here he stands, companion — family! Made from sea pottery. Otto! There you are at last.

But, I confess, after all, he worries me, too. This is not the companion I asked for. It is not him at all.

Otto? You come from all over the world. Will you not move? Show just a little life? You keep so still.

Sometimes now, when I hear a crack, I assume it is the ill-face — only to turn and see small pieces of Otto falling to the floor. My fish glue is not perfect; this place is damp.

Or perhaps it's the work of ill-face after all, pulling the pieces off.

Either way, Otto lives not. Not for me.

I had hoped he might. I put his hands out in order to let him hug. But he is a stupid, dull Otto, and he does not understand. No, he is no pine-son, no tree-life.

Do I love him, poor cold Otto, when he snubs me so, insults me?

How can I, when all my love goes to my *Pino*.

Perhaps that is why Otto cannot move.

14.

But thirty remaining.

I am in the business of doubting. Not sure exactly when this began, but it is certainly there now, pulling down upon the corners of my mouth. I am no longer certain. I get confused and wonder: Was I wrong? The caning, was that bad? The screw eye, did that hurt? But no good comes of spoiling the child.

Someone else has been writing in my book. It comes in when I sleep, it helps itself. Creeping ill-face, I fear, spilling darkness all about.

I am running out of light.

I shall be blind soon, though my eyes do yet work.

One thing I do perceive: A little boy of wood. If I close my eyes I seem to see him, but if I open them, he flees away.

■ ■ ■ ■

This morning I ventured out, out onto the main deck, hands shaking. I had a saw with me; there was good wood yet to liberate. But so much blackness now, so many roots have overtaken my ship, as if it were wrapped in dark rope.

I began by hacking at the quarterdeck. Before long, I had liberated a good piece of plain wood, flat and smooth on the underside. Solid timber. How *Maria* screamed at me as I cut into her, but I kept at it even so: with all the holes I have made upon this ship, she would hardly be ruined by another. I am the hairy woodworm! And as I heaved the wood along, the roots seemed to grow around my ankles, until there: THERE HE WAS!

Spitting at me. The ill-face! Right before me! No doubting this time. Screeching at me. Actually there, in the flesh! ROOTS SCRATCHING!

I tumbled back down the stairs, cutting myself badly, and heaved the wood beside me into the captain's chart room. I slammed the door behind me. And I listened.

Knock.

Knock.

It is outside. Branches clicking against the

door. Tap-tapping away. Toc! Toc! Chipping away at the door. And I?

I paint.

I paint him. My boy. An apology, the only way I know how.

On this board, trembling, I undertake to paint me a son. If only in two dimensions. *I am so sorry, my boy, my only!* I scream as I paint. To remember my boy, grown so human. I pray that he shall keep.

I start with the eyes, determined that he will look at me and even encourage me with his eyes. Might there be forgiveness there? Might his be eyes of kindness and approval? *Yes, Babbo,* might the eyes tell me? *Yes, Babbo: all is well?*

Twenty-five.

All is well, you do see.

How I do like to paint. How I do need to make things, to keep my mind from running out. I sit in my small pool of light, surrounded by such darkness, and I finish the work on my son. I write his name there, so that there can be no doubt: Eye of pine. Pinocchio. The wood that sees. Pine nut. *Noce.* Also *occhio,* for eye. Eye that pines.

Like the old masters, I paint him in darkness, but with the face in bright light. Twenty candles left, nineteen, seventeen. God grant that I may finish the picture before the light runs out.

But fifteen.

It shan't be long now. I make my last few entries in Harald's book while I still may. I shall fight the darkness as long as I can. Come, come, brush made of my beard. Let us go on, for God's sake. I shall do it before the always-blackness swallows.

For, you see, I am being eclipsed. Being eaten. By the encroaching one. Oh!

Ten!

I am here.

No, no, please go. I have so little time.

When the light goes, I shall remain; then shall I take over this ship. I have been nibbling at you — soft nibbles so far, small nips, little crumbs of you have I taken. But I am ravening; I have ever more hunger. I am growing teeth of length and sharpness. My jaw aches. I shall bite. Flesh come away. I shall bite and bite and bite.

Help! You are not there. I cannot see you.

I am here. I am here when the light's out. Here in this corner!

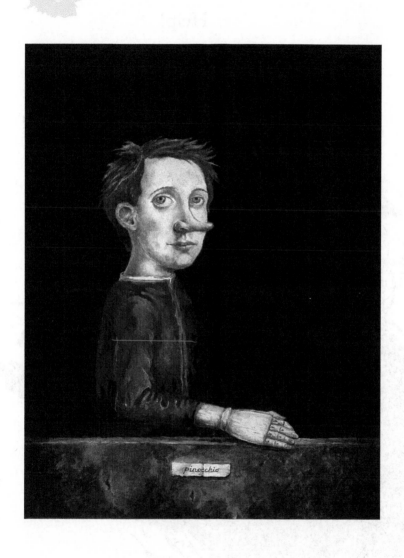

pinocchio

Oh! Go, go away. You frighten me!

I am coming.

Help!

Knock!

Knock!

Bang!

■ ■ ■ ■

The roots have come now into the chart room, spreading from ill-face, covering the walls. But I have yet possession of the cabin, and I pull myself inside. There, within, I am still a man in a room, safe a little while yet.

The bed, you see. Captain's bed. And my light. I may set light to the ill-face and all its spreading limbs. I'll make such a fire, I'll burn ill-face to death: that shall be my ending.

And yet — I know this now, I cannot avoid it — it is all my doing. To create such a blackness, it did come from me. I gave it breath. And now I create the fire that will quench it. The fire will destroy the shark, and it will set my own son free.

Ill-face is nothing like my little boy. Oh, to see him again — how his face would put the blackness out. If I could but make him once more. A boy; a great, proud boy.

I love, I would tell it.

And let it free, let it swim, let it go on.

Yet here is wood before you, old man: wood still fresh, the solid bed, the boards. The tools. Might you, with one last breath, *use it?*

I am sorry, my son. I am so *sorry.* No hooks, never no more.

I, frightened, frightened you away. Did I not?

Can I bring you back?

When ill-face taps at the door, tap tap, I reply with my toc toc at this new wood. It leads me, the wood does. It always has if I let it.

Come, I tell it, break free my sorrow. Come, I beg thee.

Still, though, Joseph: let the wood do it. Toc. Toc. Tap tap. No, no, you may not come in, you may not.

It comes now, the wood — how it comes along. I feel its sides. Not quite a boy, yet, but I shall let the wood be free. No. No! This is not right, not yet. This is no child.

Trust the wood.

Can I? Did it? Move a little. Was there? *Life?*

Come now. Yes! It wriggles in my arm! It thrashes!

There, Pino. Come, my woodling, breathe, beat.

It *moves*! It does! Look!

Tap!

Toc.

Tap! Tap!

Toc. Toc.

But no, wood, you are wrong! Wood, you mustn't. This is not feet but a tail.

A wooden tail has just slapped me in the face.

It is hard to hold back, what flippers, Pino, surely. Are you fish now?

And yet nose again — great nose, for how else can I know it is you? Come nose, nose nose. Oh, how the nose stretches out, in a spiral, to a point.

This is no wooden child I make. Look there — it has a wooden sword! Look at the weapon! Such fight in you!

Tap! Tap!

Come, hurry, there's no time. The *Maria* is splitting. Come, woodlife, I'll sharpen your sword. How it grows out of you, of your face.

Eyes, little dark eyes. See me! It lives! Oh, it LIVES!

Crash!

It is a fish! A wooden fish, but how it flaps in the captain's cabin. Water, water, it must breathe. Oh, my fishson, fishboy, fishchild. Look at you: Nose of the Sea! *Narvalo!* Pinocchio's good spirit! That is who you are. Who else could you be? A sea unicorn! A narwhal! The fish with the sharp snout! Impossible beast!

Come now, my love. Let us get you out, for the ship shall not last long. I *made*! Again!

Crack! Boom!

What a smashing! Yet at last I know my

purpose. I take hold of my wooden son, my boy come a narwhal, my own art, and I break open the door with my own strength. I hold the wooden fish close to me.

It is there! Ill-face! Just there, beyond the door, thick with his roots. How wide it opens its mouth at the gleaming wood I hold. I hold up the wooden fish, and ill-face sees it. It opens its black mouth so wide! Such a scream it makes.

And I scream back.

And my fishboy screams. A child's voice! Yes! Yes!

And along we rush, down the corridor, while the ill-face is caught in his scream-shock.

There's a great rent in the ship now, I can feel it — a terrible new collapse. She has broken in two, opened a great hole, and we come to break too fast, too fast. We slip from the edge, we fall, we tumble down in the muck, until we are all down there, upon the sharkfloor.

But wait —

I dropped him! The fish, the sharp-nosed fish!

Where, boy?

And now the ill-face is coming spidering down. Black roots creeping all about, amid shrieks of splitting wood.

Ah, but there he is! The little wooden

pinwhal, flapping hopeless in the damp. Quick, 'Petto, leap that carcass, rush your old bones. The dark branches are coming on!

Pick him up, wipe him down. Then *run*.

To the shark throat. The throat. Hurry, hurry now!

How he writhes. Soon boy, soon!

15.

I am with him, my narboy, in the throat.

It's all black. I see nothing, though I can hear the ill-face screaming for me. I heave him up, my boy the fish: Look! Look, there, the mouth, the teeth. Do you see? The shark is at the surface.

There's a sudden rush of light. TRUE LIGHT! But the water comes pouring down, pushing us back into the dark. Still, I hold on while I may.

Out, my boy! You must get out. Look — there is light beyond the teeth. Look, the light. Now! Fast! The light is going. Go, my boy, swim!

A root has me by the foot. It is tugging.

Go, life! Swim!

I kiss it.

I LET HIM GO.

Let him go, and I come tumbling back down into the belly.

I am alone again. The wooden fish is gone.

He swam free. And I tumbled down again. But faster it seemed, this time — pulled over and over, I was. And I landed, yes, upon it. Right on the ill-face.

ON ITS HEAD.

Smashed its skull in. I did, I did. What a loud crack, of a stick broken, or bones cracking. I smashed him. Broke him into pieces. It's done now, ill-face is. I have small bits of him in my hands. Crumbling, rotten wood. Ash. Nothing to see but the last of the *Maria* dying in her decay.

I have rescued some small pieces of the captain: The little chest. The journal that I may set this down, full of scraps and images.

Just two candles left.

No shiphome no more. I'll sit here. It shall be dark before long.

Last.

I am at the final candle, hovering over it, staring into the light. It is time I let go. The darkness is coming. It is nearly here.

Quite suddenly, as I write, there is some new plashing in the distance, some noise of life. Come, I'll look at it — I'll view the thrashing with my last candlelight. Poor thing, I do hear it, no doubt some fish desperate to find water and panicking. I'm sorry for thee, small beast, and for all thy brothers and sisters who took this path before. The splashing continues, it gets louder, it comes closer. Surely not the *narvalo* back? Not eaten, my wooden fishboy?

No, no, thank the lord. It is not a fish like I have seen before — yet there is something familiar in it, this new thing. A ghost? Perhaps; prepare yourself, I think, to be haunted. Yes, do get along with it, what shade of dread shall you be?

And on it does come, this vision, like nothing I have seen, yet so familiar. It is something bipedal, I can see, and fish — this is documented — have no call for legs. Who comes then? What is this? Closer and closer yet. No shade of bleached white like I, nor like other ghosts, no, no. A new haunting this is, like something fresh living. Come to blow out my light, are you, to kill my last candle?

It is here beside me now, even here as I write these words upon this page, staring at me, putting out its hands as I tremble. It feels familiar, yes, so old, known and lost, something from before, but what is its name? And then the thing speaks: a new sound, not my sound, not me doing voices, but some sound

of which I am not capable, and it says, this
unexpected being, this creature within a
creature — I shall break, I shall surely break
— it says, this effigy, this child:
"Babbo!"
And I see —
    Pinocchio PINOCCHIO PINOCCHIO

Pinocchio, oh, no.
  Go back. Go back.
          PINOCCHIO
      little pinocchio, my child
             he is come home to me
                  Pinocchio

Tunnite me and Babbo we will escayp.
  He will clime onto my back.
  I'll be his bowt.
  He is so tyred.
  We will get out tunnite.
  By. By. Going now.
  Outwerds.

AFTERWORD

BY ATHELWOLD EZEKIEL GREEM, M.D., VINALHAVEN, MAINE, U. S. A.

To the reader:

The story of the monster is well-known to the people of my island. On January 23, 1887, a sea creature the like of which was new to us, and very strange, was beached upon our land. There was no hope of saving its life, for when it landed on our shore it was already some time dead; there was plentiful evidence of rotting about its wrinkled skin. I am sorry for that, for in many ways the advanced putrefaction had robbed the monster of so much majesty: it seemed, to my mind, enfeebled as it lay helpless and expired on our common land. We did, however, make a holiday of it. The whole town came out to visit. All shops were closed. There was something extraordinary to be seen, and child and ancient alike came to be near it.

I am no exaggerator; I am a doctor. I apply myself to facts as much as any person may. But there, upon the sand, was a new fact. A fact not entered in any of the five hundred volumes of my personal library — good library though it is, and one with no small fame in this locality. People come from all corners of the island to visit my library. True, it is not a very large island. But it is very full of facts. And there, of a sudden, was a very new fact before us.

A very large fact.

Nothing this size had been previously known. Dolphins had washed up, sharks, too, even sperm whales. But this was something new. How can I say it so that you who did not see it may comprehend its enormity? It changed the very landscape, as if there were now a hill, a big hill or small mountain, where before there was none. It quite filled the beach with its corpse. A whole locomotive could have driven through the tunnel of its mouth with great ease, allowing not just the engine but four or five carriages to follow and still be contained. It changed our very conception of size. We had not known anything was capable of such amplitude. It was as if God had given us a hint of Himself. Or was this fresh evidence of Hell? We felt a chosen people. Or a cursed.

Was it real, or were we dreamers, we asked ourselves. Once we had put our hands to the creature's appalling skin, however, we could but answer that this was an absolute truth. Was this the same gross form — I have done my investigations — spotted passing through the Strait of Gibraltar in 1875? Or the immense shape recorded by the crew of the RMS *Zanoni* in the Gulf Saint Vincent? Or even the dark shadow that followed the Russian monitor *Smerch* for two whole days in the Arctic Circle? I suspect it may indeed have begat that outlandish rumor. But monsters — monsters are fact, this I know.

What were we then to do with such an unlikely spectacle?

It could not be eaten. Not without fear of illness. I estimate it must have died some weeks or even months before its arrival, and indeed there were visible bites from other sea life about it. However, while it had been sampled by other creatures, it seemed somehow to have repelled them. Thus it was left alone to roll in the ocean until at last it settled here with us. Was it a gift? Was it a punishment? Should we have boasted of it to the world or should we have covered it up?

Before we could answer these questions, it became obvious that something had to be done about our new habitant. Good or ill, it could not be left where it was. This colossus, though dead, was a danger to us.

It poisoned the air. It had been with us but

two days before this hazard began to show itself. Babies started to sleep longer and were harder to waken. Milk began to spoil within an hour of arriving at market. An old woman died while sitting on a bench in Skoog Park. Then, on the third day, we woke to discover that small spots had begun to form on the backs of our necks. Our jaws felt stiff and we complained of headaches. Our hair, in certain cases, began to fall out. Teeth did likewise, and there was a certain yellowing of our skin. Birds dropped from the sky, quite dead. Our dogs vomited in the streets, and cats hissed and fled us, fur on end.

I insisted that the island be quarantined. If all life on Vinalhaven should come to an end, far better that only our island be afflicted while all humanity beyond remain safe. Ferry service across Penobscot Bay from Rockland was abolished, as were journeys by all other craft. We excluded ourselves, for a time, from the rest of humanity.

The great fish was the cause, and that fish, once our pride, now became our terror. We had to get rid of the thing, to destroy and dismantle it, though even the stoutest among us found their strength ebbing each day. If we did not go to it soon, there would be little hope for us.

But stay a moment.

I am, as I have said, a medical man of curious mind. I knew that a simple walk around the beast would give me much information, but I required to know what was inside the deceased. This foul creature, this horror-mound, had to be opened up and fractioned, for only after we had burned it or buried it could we hope to breathe freely again. Volunteers were called for, and twenty of our strongest came forward, dressed in fishing leathers, while the remainder were told to keep indoors until the all-clear had been given.

Down we went unto the beach, with long knives and treesaws to make that one big thing into many a smaller thing. In the name of science I wished to have some knowledge of its inner workings, and so I commanded that the belly be split open and the contents drawn out. What sawing and wrenching there followed, and then what new abominable stench, but the thing was opened now and a tunnel made within the flesh. I asked who would go inside and enter the inner world of the creature, and receiving no answer — for all were in dread fear of it — I had a closed lanthorn lit and climbed in by myself.

It was a slippery road, bordered by thick walls, and I soon began to wonder about the wisdom of my adventure, about whether this doleful palace might collapse about me. Still, I went on until I reached a vast opening, like some hall or a church, and found myself within the main cavern of the creature. What a strange emptiness it was! My flame did not immediately make sense of the surroundings, but ere long it seemed to me that yonder was a familiar shape. How could it be? But true enough, there it was: A ship. Broken and rotted, and much of it burnt, yet surely once a ship, long since swallowed by the colossus. Were there, I wondered, any survivors inside? I called out, but there was no reply. Indeed, it seemed madness to hope for life within such a tomb. I went closer to the unhappy wreck then, and using a rope slung over the side, I gained access to the vessel itself. The walls were no longer of discernible wood but covered in some filth, secretions of the stomach no doubt. And so I climbed within the rotting vessel — and there I found the objects, the workings, the very museum of a single poor human soul who had evidently been trapped within, eaten and yet living, and had persisted, apparently, for some years.

How I wept then, I, a man of science — at these poor artifacts, at the fate of a fellow creature.

I looked everywhere for some piece of the

unfortunate. I called, I searched in the be-fouled cabins, but no human remainder, no slumped bag of human skin did I uncover. What bones I found — and there were many — were of fish swallowed and rotted in that gaseous hall. There was, too, a small child-like shape contrived out of pieces of broken pottery and glued together, not unartful perhaps, and no doubt precious to its maker. And heads there were, lifesize heads, made from some pale substance; and paintings on wood of recognizably human faces, some large, some quite small; and paintings on shells, too, and bone!

Thus did I make this discovery, one that brought to my mind the cave paintings of ancient man communicating with us over unthinkable distance. Here, too, was life.

On that dank morning, I resolved that every piece, small or large, of this unfor-tunate human's work must be rescued. It must be carefully removed from its place and taken to a cleaner environment where it could be preserved for permanent study. Ev-erything must be saved: The brushes made of his beard. The bone tools. The sail-canvas tablecloth. Paintings on bone, on board, on vellum. And the words in the book he left behind — the diary and the stories — I have had translated into several of the languages of the world. He wrote his stories, it seems to me, to entertain himself, to keep himself alive. I do not always understand him. His delusions of a wooden child, for instance, defy explanation. He seems also to have been frightened of his own squid-black marks upon the page, as if at times a madness gripped the pen. I have had his several objects captured by a camera device, and have positioned these pieces of evidence in the relevant places throughout this book.

The creature, alas, we burned. Such thick smoke it made. I smell it to this day.

The prisoner's work has taken up permanent residence in my own home. I have lived unencumbered since the loss of my wife and three children to smallpox, and so I have the good fortune of making this collection of a man's life the newest part of my library. I open my door so that others may come to contemplate.

I have, in the years since, tried to determine the ending of the gentleman who lived inside the fish. I did discover that the entire crew of the Danish schooner *Maria* went down with all hands somewhere near the island of Ærø in the winter of 1876, but it is clear from the surviving diary that this monster's last tenant was not among their number. I have sent out pleas in the form of advertisements in papers; I have applied to many universities and governments, no doubt causing much mirth and incredulity. You cannot live in a stomach, I have been told in so many ways. I know that — and yet. No such man living in Collodi, province of Lucca, but there was an abandoned ceramics factory there, and in a ledger was one Giuseppe Lorenzini, long since absconded, who owed many months' rent on a small municipal room. I have found no further trace of him.

Some nights I dream of that poor old man, and in my dream I am always asking him where he has gone. He has never answered me yet, but I shall keep trying.

My home has come to be known for the collection it houses and has earned a nickname. They call it "Fish House" because it has grown a smell now, like a gas, coming from these certain treasures that have made a home for themselves all over the property. As if the various objects were alive. I like the sound of this name. I have commissioned a sign for the front door:

THE FISH HOUSE

There, then, we are a regular museum. We are open Monday to Saturday, 10:00 a.m. until 4:00 p.m. Sundays closed for prayer.

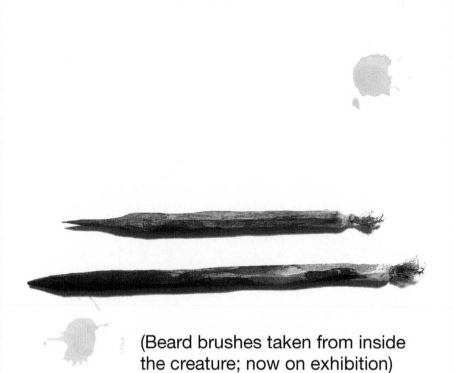

(Beard brushes taken from inside
the creature; now on exhibition)

ACKNOWLEDGMENTS

I would like to thank David Goodrich and his fine beard, some of which he donated; Lisa Olstein for being chief hair procurer; Mia Carter for the timely delivery of mussel shells; Diana Cherbuliez for sending the perfect fishing net; Lucy Marco and Susan Adams for the generous gift of red hairs from their heads; Dana Burton for her scanning brilliance; Nick Cabrera for his wonderful eye and splendid photographs; my ever-wonderful agent and friend Isobel Dixon; and James Pusey, Hana Murrell, Emanuela Anechoum, Sian Ellis-Martin, and the whole team at Blake Friedmann for their work and support of this book in London and abroad; Valeria Ioele, Eugenio Lio, and Emma Paoli for their work on this book and its accompanying exhibition in Italy; Gregory Norminton for his careful and inspired advice; Michael Taeckens for his invaluable support; Marguerite White for boxes and boxes of brilliant detritus from the shores of Massachusetts; and my beloved Gus and Matilda for finding the best possible pieces of pottery washed up on the beaches of Provincetown, the harbor of Tobermory, and the Thames foreshore.

I am grateful to the Fondazione Nazionale Carlo Collodi in allowing me to exhibit at the Parco di Pinocchio in Collodi. This book would not have happened without the spark from two incredible people: Elisabetta Sgarbi and Alba Donati. Alba came up with the idea for the exhibition, and Elisabetta immediately agreed to publish the words that now belong to it.

Since the book was published in Italian it has changed and grown as it readied itself for publication in English. I am enormously grateful for those that made that possible: the brilliant team at great Gallic who have become my very happy British home — especially the outstanding duo Jane Aitken and Emily Boyce; Maddy Allen, Polly Mackintosh, Isabelle Flynn, and the marvelous Sophie Goodfellow at FMcM; and to the amazing people at Riverhead, particularly Glory Plata, Catalina Trigo, Jynne Martin, Geoffrey Kloske, and the long-suffering and ever-wise and inspiring man in the whale beside me, Mr. Calvert Morgan.

Lastly, and mostly, to Elizabeth, who, some years ago now, came and got me out.

ABOUT THE AUTHOR

Edward Carey is a novelist, visual artist, and playwright. His previous novels include *Little, Alva & Irva,* and *Observatory Mansions,* and an acclaimed series for young adults, the Iremonger Trilogy. His writing for the stage includes an adaptation of Robert Coover's *Pinocchio in Venice,* a continuation of the Pinocchio story. Born in England, he now teaches at the University of Texas in Austin, where he lives with his wife, the author Elizabeth McCracken, and their family.